A King Production presents…

All I See Is The Money…

Female Hustler 5

A Novel

JOY DEJA KING

Cover concept by Joy Deja King
Cover model: Joy Deja King
Library of Congress Cataloging-in-Publication Data;

A King Production
Female Hustler Part 5/by Joy Deja King

For complete Library of Congress Copyright info visit;

www.joydejaking.com
Twitter: @joydejaking

A King Production
P.O. Box 912, Collierville, TN 38027

A King Production and the above portrayal logo are trademarks of A King Production LLC.

This Book is Dedicated To My:

Family, Readers, and Supporters.
I LOVE you guys so much. Please believe that!!

—Joy Deja King

"The Devil Whispered In My Ear,
"You're Not Strong Enough
To Withstand The Storm..."

"I Whispered Back, "I Am The Storm..."

Aaliyah

A KING PRODUCTION

All I See Is The Money…

Female Hustler 5

A Novel

JOY DEJA KING

Chapter One

When Doves Cry

Aaliyah stood stoically, watching the fairytale life she'd envisioned having with Dale, dissolve right before her eyes. Dale's hand was steady and firm as he continued aiming his gun directly at her family while taunting Aaliyah.

"You betta decide who's gonna die first before I decide for you!" Dale spit to a shaken Aaliyah.

"Dale...please! I'm begging you not to do this. It's not too late. We can still get married and make this work," she cried but Dale wasn't trying to hear it.

"What the fuck don't you get! I'm done wit' you. You ain't gon' neva be my wife. Now I'ma ask you one last time. Who you gon' sacrifice first? Your mother," Dale said pointing the gun at Precious. "Nico," he then moved the gun to point at him, "Or fuckin' Supreme. The one responsible for murdering my brother." Dale had nothing but rage in his eyes. Aaliyah didn't even recognize the man she wanted to spend the rest of her life with.

"Dale, this is between me and you," Supreme stood up and said. "Let my daughter go and everyone else here too. If you want to kill somebody, kill me but don't cause unnecessary bloodshed because of your anger over what I did."

"Supreme, what are you doing?!" Precious mouthed, pulling on his arm.

"Over what you did?" Dale leaned back and scowled up his face. "Nigga, you killed my brother."

"No, I was trying to save my daughter's life. Your brother was working with Maya and Arnez.

He was well aware they were holding Aaliyah hostage. The woman you claim to love. But instead of him telling you where she was, he chose to remain silent. Your brother was no victim but my daughter was. If you wanna kill me for protecting my child then so be it because I would do it again."

Dale's eyes darted back and forth between Supreme and Aaliyah before resting on his rejected bride to be. For a brief moment, Dale seemed to loosen his grip on the gun as if having second thoughts. He was incensed but seeing how distraught and defeated Aaliyah appeared to be, got to him but Dale fought against it. He didn't want to soften up, he wanted to hold on to his reason to kill.

"Dale, I should've told you the truth but I was scared you wouldn't understand and I would lose you."

"What, you tryna blame me?!" Dale scoffed.

"No! But it isn't my fault what happened to Emory and it isn't my father's fault either. He was trying to find me before Maya and Arnez had a chance to kill me."

"I don't believe you or Supreme!" he shouted. "Emory had no reason to work with Maya or Arnez and he knew how I felt about you. My brother wouldn't have sat back and let me go crazy worrying about you, if he had any fuckin' clue where you were. You shittin' on my brother's name to save yo' father's life but it ain't gonna work!" Dale's voice seemed to echo loudly through the distraught crowd.

"We have to do something," Precious whispered to both Supreme and Nico who were sitting beside her.

"In case you haven't noticed, Dale came prepared," Nico groaned. "He has a fuckin' small army with him and they all got heat while we ain't got shit," he seethed.

"So, what we're supposed to sit here and let Dale kill us and our daughter?" Precious fumed.

"We're not dead yet and I have no plans for us to die anytime soon," Supreme stated, while calculating what their next move should be. The more he mulled over their options, he realized they didn't have any. Supreme became completely enthralled in his thoughts, it wasn't until two men grabbed him, did he realize what was going on.

"Let him go!" Precious jumped up and screamed. One of the men holding Supreme's arm, pointed his gun in Precious's face letting her know to back the fuck up.

"Precious, sit down." Nico insisted, pulling her back down in the chair.

"I can't let them kill my husband," Precious wailed.

"Husband?! You and Supreme are married?" Nico questioned, looking dumbfounded.

"Yes." Precious revealed. "I didn't mean to blurt it out," she shook her head while keeping Supreme in her sight.

"When did this happen?"

"A few weeks ago. We wanted to wait until after Aaliyah's wedding to tell everyone."

"Why all the secrecy?" Nico inquired.

Precious turned and sulked at Nico before responding. "It wasn't that serious," she snapped. "We've been married before and did the big wedding production. We wanted something simple and private. Can we discuss this later? We have bigger problems right now...like saving Supreme's life."

She felt herself becoming sick at the very idea of losing her daughter and husband. But with the glare in Dale's eyes, Precious knew all of their lives were in jeopardy.

"I don't think there's any saving Supreme," Nico shrugged. "Dale appears to be determined to get retribution for his brother's murder."

"You want Supreme to die," Precious said, becoming furious. "You do know Dale isn't going to stop with Supreme. His intent is to kill all of us," she reminded Nico.

"When you put it like that I guess…"

"You guess…?!" Precious shook her head, grasping how Nico's dislike for Supreme ran deeper than she realized.

"What are you doing? I can't let you kill my father," Aaliyah sobbed when two of Dale's goons posted Supreme next to them.

"Dale, please let my daughter go. Aaliyah shouldn't have to watch you kill her father," Supreme reasoned.

"Look at you, still tryna play the champion, even with death knocking at yo' door," Dale chuckled. "I don't give a fuck!" he said, itching to burn a hole through Supreme's chest.

"I'm begging you!" Aaliyah shrieked. "Pleeeeease don't kill my father."

"Would you rather me kill Precious or Nico first? The choice is yours."

"Telling you which one of my parents to

shoot first isn't a choice, it's a death sentence to the people I love. This isn't who you are, Dale. You're not a monster."

"She's right, man. You're not a monster." Desmond stood up from his chair and started walking towards Dale. A few of his gunmen were about to step in and stop Desmond but Dale put his hand up, letting them know he was cool.

"Desmond, we go way back but you need to stay outta this. This ain't yo' beef," Dale told him.

"What is Desmond doing," Justina mumbled under her breath.

"Trying to get Dale to end this craziness," Angel mumbled back. "Hopefully he's convincing."

"Dale is completely unstable. What if Desmond gets himself killed," Justina said becoming panic stricken.

"Are those tears I see in your eyes?" Angel remarked as Justina tried to wipe them away. "You really care about him, don't you?" she questioned sounding stunned.

"I love him. Now please stop talking to me. I want to hear what he's saying to Dale," Justina huffed, focusing her attention on the two men. They stepped away and seemed to be in a deep conversation. Although Dale was busy talking to

Desmond, it didn't matter because he left strict instructions with his goons, to shoot anyone who moved.

"Who is that man speaking to Dale and what do you think he's saying?" Precious whispered to Nico.

"That's Desmond Blackwell. He's in the same line of business as me but also owns a few very successful nightclubs. From my understanding, he's extremely close to Dale. Desmond's the one who threw their engagement party," Nico explained to Precious. "Maybe he can convince his friend a bloody massacre ain't the way to go," he stated evenly.

Precious didn't understand how Nico could remain so calm under their dire circumstances. It took every ounce of self control she had, not to run up on Dale. But having a gunman standing a few feet away, ready to put a bullet in her head, motivated Precious to exercise it and remain seated.

"Dale, you can't do this. I understand your pain. That was your brother. I had a lot of love for Emory too but killing Supreme and the rest of Aaliyah's family on what was supposed to be your wedding day, is suicide," Desmond warned.

"What you mean suicide?" Dale questioned.

"Say you kill all them people today...then what?" Desmond nodded his head. "You wanna spend the rest of your life on the run? Because your life is over. You'll either end up dead, when they people retaliate, or you'll die in jail once you get caught."

Dale knew everything Desmond said was correct but it didn't stop him from battling his conscious. He was torn and that was obvious to everyone observing the two men's interaction.

"Why did it have to be my brother?!" Dale bit down on his lip fighting the tears ready to escape his eyes. From the moment, he remembered what Nesa told him, Dale had been keeping his pain bottled up inside. He never properly mourned the death of his brother because he was determined not to let Aaliyah know he knew the truth. This only ignited his anger and pain to further build, until it was ready to erupt like a smoldering volcano.

"I know, man," Desmond patted Dale on the shoulder empathizing with his anguish. "Death ain't nothing nice but Emory wouldn't want you to go out like this."

"You right, he wouldn't," Dale admitted. He

turned and faced Aaliyah. Her perfectly done makeup had been ruined, as it was completely smeared from her steady sobbing. Guilt began to creep up on Dale, witnessing the devastation he caused the woman he had been madly in love with. He lowered his gun, realizing he needed to take Desmond's advice. But then one of his goons who was holding Supreme coughed, which made Dale turn in that direction. Resting his eyes on the man responsible for murdering his brother, once again triggered the flame that had almost burnt out.

"Fuck that shit! You gon' die motherfucker!" Dale howled, lifting his gun back up.

"Don't do it!" Desmond shouted, jumping in front of Dale to try and get the gun out of his hand but it was too late. The shot was fired and chaos ensued.

Chapter Two

Back In The USA

Taren's flight landed in Miami the morning of Aaliyah's wedding. Although she had started a new life in Mexico, social media made it possible for her to stay in the loop, by stalking Angel and her inner circle online. Angel didn't post much but her newfound sister was a different story. Aaliyah loved to share her every move. So, when she posted a picture of her, Justina and Angel with the tagline, preparing for the most important day of my life, with her maids of honor getting alterations for their dresses to her upcoming wedding, Taren began plotting.

Taren would check not only Aaliyah's but Darien's snapchat multiple times a day. Once she learned the date of Aaliyah's upcoming nuptials and that Darien Blaze would be in Vegas training for his upcoming fight, Taren knew this was the perfect opportunity for her to sneak back in town and make her move.

"I'm here to check into my room," Taren said to the older man behind the counter.

"I'll be happy to help you. Can I please get the name your reservation is under?"

"Nikki Thompson."

"Yes, here you are Miss Thompson. All I need is your driver's license and credit card."

"Here you go." Taren handed the man her fake ID and credit card which was nothing short of pristine. The man didn't flinch and Taren wasn't the least bit surprised. Being the con artist that she was, Taren quickly hooked up with some unsavory men who had the credit card scam on lock. Mix in a tad bit of drug trafficking and Taren found herself a nice little hustle to keep her funds flowing. She hadn't put so much as a dent in the money she'd tricked Angel out of.

"Here's your room key, on the top floor with an ocean view as requested," the man grinned widely. Having no clue that everything about the woman standing in front of him was fake. From the ID, credit card, hair and even her recently purchased breasts. Taren was a brand new woman and she planned on using it to her advantage.

"A lady by the name of Clarissa is here to see you," Mrs. Armstrong said walking into Dominique's room.

"Finally!" Dominique beamed, jumping off her bed but Mrs. Armstrong blocked her from exiting out the door. "Is there a reason why you're standing in my way?" she asked curiously.

"Mr. Blackwell never gave clearance for this Clarissa woman to come over," Mrs. Armstrong stated, not budging. She was an older lady, but tall and sturdy. Physically, she easily outmatched the very petite Dominique.

"Mrs. Armstrong, relax. I sent Desmond a text earlier today, asking him if it was okay for

Clarissa to stop by. She works at one of his clubs. I swear!" Dominique insisted but her watchdog was not convinced. "I can show you the text," she huffed, going back over to the bed to retrieve her phone.

Mrs. Armstrong raised an eyebrow as she read their text exchange. "That's unlike Mr. Black-well. He's usually very good at alerting me to any visitors allowed to come over."

"You know that huge wedding is today. He probably got busy and forgot to call you," Dominique reminded her, feeling sad.

"The wedding you were supposed to attend as his date. I didn't realize that was today. No wonder you've been moping around here all day."

"I haven't been moping," Dominique sulked, glancing up at Mrs. Armstrong. "Maybe a little."

"No need to deny it. I would be moping too if I thought I had a chance with a fine man like that, only to find out he's taken," the bossy caretaker smacked.

"Thanks a lot! You're not making me feel any better."

"I said he was taken, not married. He ain't walked down the aisle yet," Mrs. Armstrong winked. "You've kept your friend waiting long enough.

Hopefully some girl talk will turn that frown into a smile."

"Thanks!" Mrs. Armstrong wasn't the affectionate type but that didn't stop Dominique from giving her a quick hug before running off to the living room to see Clarissa.

"Hey Girl!" Clarissa stood up from the couch and smiled when Dominique came skipping in.

"You don't know how happy I am to see you!" Dominique gushed, squeezing Clarissa tightly. "Come on, let's go sit outside on the balcony, so we can have a little privacy."

"You look great. How are you feeling?" Clarissa asked, sitting down on one of the chairs.

"Good," Dominique said, closing the glass door before sitting down. "I would be great if I didn't feel like such a prisoner."

"I ain't neva seen no jails that are this plush," Clarissa cracked. "Desmond has you living right. Lucky girl."

"I guess I should feel lucky. If it wasn't for Desmond hiding me out, I'd probably met the same fate as Aspen."

"I can't believe Aspen is gone. Her phone hasn't been cut off yet, so I still call sometimes just to hear her voicemail," Clarissa admitted.

"She sounds so bubbly and full of life."

"You all were super close. I know losing her has to be difficult. No matter how hard I try to forget it, the sound of that gunshot continues to ring in my head. Then Taren keeping me caged up like an animal, before leaving me to die in the explosion. I think that's why it's so hard for me to stay in this condo. It reminds me how trapped I felt when she had me tied up in the closet, at her apartment," Dominique sighed.

"Man, Taren is a piece of work. That heifa has a serious ass whoopin' coming her way." Clarissa shook her head. "I can't believe ain't nobody tracked her trifling ass down yet."

"The last update Desmond gave me, she was in Texas or someplace far from here."

"I bet! She ain't that crazy. Taren don't have a death wish and coming back to Miami would guarantee her being six feet under," Clarissa popped.

"You ain't lying. Desmond is determined to find her. It's consuming him," Dominique said with uneasiness. "I don't think he'll get a good-night sleep until Taren is dead."

"You over there sounding like a worried girlfriend instead of a concerned friend," Clarissa remarked. "Have you bonded with our boss in other ways...do tell. I mean, who would blame you."

"I wish."

"Then I'm right! You do have a crush on Desmond...I knew it!"

"I do but he has a girlfriend. She's a real bad bitch and I'm not talking about in a good way."

"You met her?"

"Yes. She came over here hurling all sorts of threats at me. She even had the nerve to push me down."

"I hope you slapped the shit outta her," Clarissa said, getting hyped.

"No. I just wanted her to get out. Plus, as angry as she was, I don't think I would've won that fight. With the rage in her eyes, she was ready to draw blood," Dominique frowned, playing with her ponytail.

"That means she sees you as a threat. Why else would she be so upset?"

"Or maybe she's simply playing mind games with Desmond and it worked."

"Mind games, what do you mean?"

"There's this big, fancy wedding going on to-day and..."

"OMG, you must be talking about that girl Aaliyah, Supreme's daughter," Clarissa jumped in and said. "Sorry, I didn't mean to cut you off but I'm a huge fan of Supreme. I listen to his music when I'm working out," she laughed. "It's old but better than most of this new rap shit out here. One of the blogs I read, mentioned his daughter was having this elaborate wedding here in Miami today. I would've loved to be there."

"Me too and I almost was," Dominique hissed.

"What happened?"

"Desmond had invited me to go. He even hired a stylist and everything. He felt bad I'd been stuck in this crib twenty-four, seven. Somehow his girlfriend found out and went ballistic. She completely shut it down. The next day he came over and said he couldn't take me. Just like that I was disinvited."

"Woah."

"Woah, is right. Maybe he was trying to make her jealous. Once it worked, he had no use for me," Dominique reasoned.

"I don't know Desmond like that but he doesn't come across as the type to play those type of games. Honestly, from the few times I have spoken to him, he ain't the type to play wit' at all."

"That's what I thought but after meeting his girlfriend, I don't know what to think. I would never expect him to be with a woman like that."

"Did you ask him why he was with her?" Clarissa questioned.

"I did. He said their relationship was complicated. He also said he loved her and from the look in Desmond's eyes, he meant it. I'll never understand how some of the craziest women get the best men," Dominique pouted.

"I know what you mean," Clarissa agreed, while reading an alert that popped on her phone. "No way!" she screamed.

"What is it...what happened?!" Dominique yelled, seeing the shocked look on her friend's face.

"I get alerts from one of the gossip sites I follow. Someone got shot at Aaliyah's wedding. Early reports are saying it's her father Supreme and his wounds might be fatal!" Clarissa uttered.

"Are you serious!" Dominique covered her mouth, taken aback by what Clarissa said. "Omigosh, does it say if anyone else being hurt? What if something happened to Desmond."

"It doesn't mention anyone else getting shot but you never know," Clarissa said while continuing to read.

"Let me call Desmond to make sure he's okay. He's not answering," she said nervously while sending him a text message.

"Come on, let's go!" Clarissa said grabbing her purse.

"Where are we going?"

"To find out exactly what happened. I have a cousin who works at a hospital. If Supreme wasn't taken there, then trust me she'll know where."

"What do I tell Mrs. Armstrong? She has strict instructions not to let me leave."

"Do you wanna find out if Desmond is okay?"

"Of course!" Dominique exclaimed.

"Then let's go. Worry about your gatekeeper when you return."

Dominique didn't even hesitate. She needed to make sure Desmond hadn't been hurt. If that meant sneaking out and not telling Mrs. Armstrong bye, then so be it.

Chapter Three

Bad At Love

"Out of all the fucked up things to happen in my life, if this isn't the worse, it's mos def top three," Aaliyah cried. "Instead of being at my reception, I'm at the emergency room, standing in my wedding dress," she fumed.

Would you please shut the fuck up! Justina wanted to scream but instead she paced the floor hoping to get an update soon. "What's taking the nurse so long to come back out? This waiting is driving me crazy."

"Both of you try to calm down," Angel said keeping her cool. She knew Aaliyah and Justina were both upset for different reasons so remaining composed was critical.

"How can I stay calm after what happened to me? And look at my makeup. My tears have completely ruined it," Aaliyah complained after catching a glimpse of her reflection in the glass behind the front desk.

"Aaliyah, you look fine." Angel tried to reassure her.

"No, I don't but I have bigger issues to worry about right now," Aaliyah scoffed. "Justina, remember when the cops question you, we didn't see who pulled the trigger."

"How can I forget!" Justina snapped. "You reminded us every two minutes on the drive over here."

"I'm only trying to make sure we have our story straight."

"I can't believe you want to protect Dale after what he did!" Justina popped.

"Keep your voice down," Aaliyah warned Justina. "The bullet only grazed my dad's arm.

My mother is with him now and the doctor said he'll be fine."

"What about Desmond!" Justina shouted. "If he doesn't make it through surgery, Dale's the blame!" Justina spit before storming off.

"Gosh, what's her deal." Aaliyah rolled her eyes before flopping down on the chair. "I didn't even know her and Desmond were friends like that. I feel horrible about what happened to him. Desmond saved my father's life but I really think it was an accident."

"Accident?" Angel side eyed Aaliyah.

"I know Dale was upset but Desmond had calmed him down. Then for some reason, he seemed to become enraged again but..."

"Aaliyah, I have to admit, I'm surprised you're trying to protect Dale. If Desmond hadn't taken that bullet, Supreme would be the one having emergency surgery right now."

"Don't you think I know that!" Aaliyah pressed her eyes shut and bit down on her lip. "I'm devastated but I can't just stop loving him. I'm supposed to be Mrs. Dale Clayborn right now," she shook her head feeling distraught. "Plus..." her voice trailed off.

"Plus, what?" Angel asked.

"I'm pregnant. I was going to surprise Dale with the news on our honeymoon," she cried.

"I'm so sorry, Aaliyah but it'll be okay," Angel said, stroking her sister's hair as she cried on her shoulder.

"I don't understand how I woke up this morning feeling like the luckiest girl in the world, to now wondering how my life has become a nightmare. It doesn't seem fair."

"It may not feel like it right now but things will get better. The more you embrace the pain, the sooner you'll heal," Angel said, speaking from her own personal experiences.

"Angel, you're the only person who knows I'm pregnant," Aaliyah said lifting her head up. "Please don't tell anyone yet."

"Of course. I promise, I won't say a word."

"Thank you," Aaliyah said wiping away her tears. "This was supposed to be the happiest day of my life. Marrying the man, I love and also carrying his baby." Aaliyah glanced down at her stomach and placed her hand over it. "Now, Dale hates me and I'm positive he's not gonna want to have anything to do with me, or our child."

"You don't know that. The agony of losing his brother is still fresh for Dale but in time he'll realize none of this was your fault."

"I should've told him the truth. He would've been upset at first but eventually, he would've forgiven my father."

"Aaliyah, don't do this to yourself. You'll go crazy." Before Angel could continue, they were interrupted.

"Hey!" Amir's appearance caught them both off guard. "I heard Supreme is gonna be fine. How you holding up, Aaliyah?" he asked taking her hand.

"How do you think?!" she hissed. "I'm sorry, Amir. I didn't mean to snap at you."

"Yes, you did but it's cool," Amir smiled sweetly. "When you're mad, it's natural to snap at the people, who you know love you the most."

"You're right. I don't know what I would do without you." Aaliyah stood up and hugged Amir tightly. "You and Justina will always be my best friends."

"No doubt. Speaking of Justina, where is she? She's not answering her phone and I wanted to take her home."

"She walked over that way," Aaliyah pointed.

"Cool. I'll be back to check on you before we leave," Amir said walking off to find Justina.

"Amir really cares about you," Angel commented after he was gone.

"The feeling is mutual. We have a lot of history. At one time, I thought if I married anyone, it would be Amir," Aaliyah let out a slight laugh. "Now he's going to marry Justina. It's crazy how our lives have changed."

"Yes, it is," Angel nodded, turning her head in the direction Amir had went. She couldn't help but wonder how his conversation with Justina was going.

"There you are!" Amir grinned when he saw Justina standing over by the vending machine. "I was worried about you."

"What are you doing here?" she asked surprised to see him.

"I came to get you. I know you wanted to ride with Aaliyah to make sure her father was okay but Supreme is fine, so I'm here to take you home."

Justina fidgeted with opening the top on her juice. She appeared to be anxious but Amir had no clue as to the reason why. "You can go ahead and leave. I'll meet you back at the apartment later on. I want to stay here."

"Aaliyah will be fine without you. She has

Angel. Last night when I got in, you were sleep. This morning you left early to meet Aaliyah at her hotel. I want us to spend some time together before I have to leave."

"You're leaving already? But you just got here."

"I know but before all that drama went down at the wedding, I had a conversation with my father."

"Isn't he on some romantic around the world trip with your mother?" Justina asked.

"Yeah, but they're headed home. A serious issue came up and I need to be back in New York by the time they arrive. You should come with me."

"I don't think that's a good idea."

"Why not? Now that this wedding is over... well it never really had a chance to start," Amir shrugged. "The point is, there's no reason for you to stay now. Your presence is no longer needed in Miami. You belong in New York with me."

"Amir, I don't know how to tell you this but..."

"Miss!" Justina turned her head with the quickness, when she heard the nurse trying to get her attention. She rushed off leaving Amir standing in the corner.

"Yes." Justina's eyes widened with fear, anticipating the worse.

"Mr. Blackwell is out of surgery and everything went well. He's expected to make a full recovery."

"Thank goodness! Can I see him?"

"He's still resting but as soon as the doctor says it's okay, I'll come get you," the nurse assured Justina.

"Okay, I'll be right here. Thank you so much," Justina said with sincerity.

"Who is Mr. Blackwell and why are you so fuckin' pressed to see him?" Amir demanded to know. Justina didn't notice Amir standing right behind her, listening to her conversation with the nurse.

"I didn't want you to find out like this but it's best I tell you now."

"Tell me what?!" Amir barked as his jaw tightened up.

"Our relationship isn't working. I don't think we need to be together."

"Hold the fuck up." Amir stepped back and eyed Justina from head to toe. She was still wearing her peach colored bridesmaid dress which gave her an angelic glow, but there was nothing innocent about the words coming out of her mouth. "Are you breaking up with me?" he could barely get the question out.

"You don't have to put it like that."

"What other way is there to put it? You kissed me goodbye this morning like shit was sweet. Now you literally telling me bye, it's over...just like that." Amir shrugged his shoulders. "What sort of bullshit game are you playin' wit' me, Justina? If this supposed to be like a joke...stop that shit now, cause it ain't funny. You see, I'm not laughing."

"Listen, it isn't something I planned." Justina's thoughts seemed to drift off. For a brief second, she reflected back to the very first day she met Desmond and was instantly drawn to him. "I have feelings for someone else."

"You've been cheating on me?!" Amir's anger had now turned to disbelief. "You been in Miami this entire time fuckin' around on me! Who is he?"

"It doesn't matter."

"Oh, yes the fuck it does. Who the hell is he?!" Amir's voice had become brash and belligerent.

"Amir, you need to keep you voice down!" Aaliyah ran over and said, as everyone in the waiting room was staring at them. "What is going on over here?"

"Justina just confessed she's been cheating on me with some Mr. Blackwell motherfucker!" Amir spit.

"Desmond?" Aaliyah revealed, simply out of shock. "You've been seeing Desmond Blackwell? It makes sense why you've had a pissy attitude since we got here."

Justina wanted to smack the shit out of Aaliyah for announcing to Amir who her mystery man was but at this point it didn't matter.

"Desmond, the nightclub owner me and Nico met with? That's who you been fuckin'!"

"We're not fuckin', we're in love," Justina stated.

"In love!" Aaliyah and Amir both said simultaneously.

"Yes. In love. It just happened."

"Oh, so you just fell on top of this nigga's dick and now you in love. Get the fuck outta here," Amir shot back. Justina looked away, trying to tune Amir out as he continued to interrogate her. She noticed the nurse calling her over and figured it must be news regarding Desmond.

"I thought you and Aaliyah would be more

understanding of my situation. I mean, Amir, you were in a relationship with me, when you cheated with my best friend. Did Aaliyah just so happen to land on your dick too?"

"Are you really..."

Justina put up her hand, cutting Amir off mid sentence. "The nurse is calling me. I'm sure it's about Desmond. Excuse me," she said walking off.

"Amir, Justina was so out of line. I'm sorry," Aaliyah said putting her hand on his shoulder.

"Don't touch me!" Amir brushed Aaliyah's hand away.

"What's your problem? You can't possibly be mad at me because of what Justina said. That was a long time ago. We both could've handled the situation better," Aaliyah spat becoming defensive.

"If you hadn't dragged Justina to Miami to be with you, she would've never gotten involved wit' this other nigga."

"I didn't drag Justina here!" Aaliyah barked back.

"Yes, you did. That's what you do, Aaliyah. You always need people around to stroke your ego. Justina should've been in New York with me.

Instead she was here being your personal lap-dog."

"No, Amir. Actually, she was here getting fucked by a man who wasn't you," Aaliyah cracked with a smug look on her face.

"You know what. I better leave now before I say something that cuts real deep." The fury in Amir's eyes cut deep enough for Aaliyah, as she watched him walk off not saying another word to her.

Chapter Four

Forgiveness

"What was all that commotion over there about?" Angel asked when Aaliyah sat down.

"This day is getting crazier by the minute and it ain't even over yet." Aaliyah rested her head on her hand. "Can you believe Justina is seeing Desmond. She claims they're in love, at least that's what she just told Amir and me."

"Wow, Justina admitted that...I didn't think she would."

"You knew?" Aaliyah gasped. "Why didn't you tell me?"

"I had an idea but it wasn't confirmed until right before the wedding started," Angel explained. "I saw them together and asked Desmond. He was very protective of her. I thought maybe it was one sided and Justina was playing him but I guess I was wrong."

"I can't believe Justina was carrying on this relationship with Desmond all this time and kept me in the dark about it. Maybe she was afraid I would tell Amir."

"Would you have?" Angel was interested in hearing Aaliyah's response.

"That's a tough one. They're both my best friends but Justina's my girl. I would've had her back. Now I feel a little guilty."

"Why?"

"Because I demanded she lie to the police for me to protect Dale. Not realizing Justina was becoming unhinged because of her close relationship to Desmond. If someone almost killed the man I love, I wouldn't want to protect him either."

"You didn't know."

"But you did. That's why you were trying to calm me down and not press Justina so much.

I'm so consumed with my own situation, I'm oblivious to everyone else's feelings." Aaliyah was waiting for her sister to respond but she seemed preoccupied. "Angel, are you even listening to me?"

"I'm sorry but I feel like I just saw a ghost," Angel mumbled.

Aaliyah turned to see who her sister was looking at. She only noticed two girls walking in. "Do you know them?"

"Yes. That's Dominique. The girl I thought died in the club explosion. Desmond told me he was hiding her out until he could locate Taren but I haven't seen her since that night. I'ma go talk to her," Angel said getting up.

"I'll come with you," Aaliyah said right by Angel's side.

"Dominique!" Angel called out. The women both stopped, appearing to be startled.

"OMG! Are you Supreme's daughter!" Clarissa yelled when she saw Aaliyah approaching in her wedding dress.

"Why, do you know my father?" Aaliyah popped.

"No, I'm just a fan. Sorry if I came off a little aggressive," Clarissa said feeling embarrassed.

"Aren't you the girl who gave me Nesa's phone number?" Angel asked, recognizing her face.

"Yes. That's me. We spoke at the club."

"Have you heard from Nesa? We were supposed to meet up and I haven't been able to get in touch with her." Even though Angel told Nico she would leave the Nesa situation alone, her gut instinct wouldn't let it rest.

"No, I haven't. The last time I heard from Nesa was the same day I spoke to you."

"I see," Angel said, then smiling at Dominique. "You probably don't remember me, but I was with you the night of the explosion. I was really worried about you. It's good to see you're doing so well."

"My memory of what happened that night is still shaky but yes, I remember you holding my hand."

"I'm sorry, I had to leave you but I'm glad you got out safely," Angel said warmly.

"Me too and thank you for being there for me. Desmond told me you're the one who pulled me away from the bomb. I would've died if it wasn't for you."

"Me too," Aaliyah added, squeezing Angel's arm.

"You saved a lot of lives that night," Clarissa

remarked, "Including Nesa's."

"If you see Nesa or if she calls, can you please tell her to get in touch with me?" Angel requested giving Clarissa her number.

"Of course. If you don't mind me asking, is Supreme okay?" Clarissa inquired. "It's all over the news and social media that he was shot."

"My father is fine. The bullet only grazed his arm."

"What about Desmond?" Dominique jumped in and asked.

Angel and Aaliyah glanced at each other awkwardly. They both hesitated before answering Dominique's question.

"Uh-oh, here comes trouble," Angel mumbled.

"What the hell are you doing here?!" Justina snapped when she saw Dominique standing with the other women.

"I heard about the shooting and I came to make sure Desmond was okay," Dominque stepped forward and told Justina.

"Well, you can turn around and walk right back out the door. When Desmond wakes up, the only person he is going to see is me."

"Wake up...does that mean Desmond was hurt...is he okay?"

With each question that rolled off Dominique's tongue, the more incensed Justina became.

"I think you should go," Angel suggested. "If anything comes up, I'll let you know. Let me walk you out." Angel wanted to hurry Dominique out but she had other ideas.

"I'm not going anywhere. I have every right to be here. Desmond is a very close friend of mine," Dominique stressed, resting her eyes on Justina. "In case you've forgotten, I'm living at his condo. And last I checked, you aren't his wife."

"This is about to get ugly," Aaliyah frowned.

"Come on, Dominique." Clarissa reached over to grab her arm so they could leave but she was already up in Justina's face.

"You think because we're in a public place, I won't drag yo' ass across this floor. Not only will I drag you, I will stomp the fuck outta you too," Justina threatened.

"Okay, we're done here," Aaliyah made clear stepping in between the women.

"I just wanna make sure Desmond is okay and then I'll leave." Dominique stood firm.

"You pressing yo' luck you little hussy!" Justina roared, reaching around Angel and yanking

Dominique up by her ponytail.

"Get yo' hands off her!" Clarissa yelled coming to her friend's rescue. But Justina was too quick. With one hand, she was holding on tightly to Dominique's hair, with the other, she smooshed Clarissa's face when she got too close.

"Oh, hell nah! You beggin' for a lashing," Clarissa popped, tossing her purse down ready to go twelve rounds with Justina.

"Everybody stop!" Angel yelled, done with trying to keep her cool. "Aaliyah, you hold Justina," she said forcing her to release the firm grip on Dominique's ponytail. "Clarissa and Dominique, both of you need to go. I'll call you as soon as I get any updates on Desmond's condition."

Both women were now hyped and ready to exchange blows with Justina but common sense kicked in. "Fine, we'll leave." Dominique agreed reluctantly.

"Thank you." Angel's voice was full of relief. "I promise to call you the moment I get any news."

"Thank you. I would greatly appreciate that," Dominque said, as Angel practically pushed the duo out the door while Aaliyah was trying to play peacemaker with Justina.

"Girl, what the hell is wrong with you?!" Aaliyah sighed. "First Amir now Dominique. If you keep this up, they're gonna throw you out."

Justina spent the next few minutes fuming before she even addressed Aaliyah. Dominique had a way of getting under her skin. She wanted to chase her down and commence to beating Dominique's ass but she knew it would only garner sympathy for the petite beauty, so Justina pulled it together.

"How dare she show up here. That broad knows I'm Desmond's girlfriend," Justina scoffed.

"I get you're territorial over your man but Dominique appeared to be genuinely concerned for Desmond. Clearly, they're friends," Aaliyah reasoned.

"Please! That two-bit stripper is nothing more than a charity case for Desmond. It's so obvious she's in love with him. She has a lot of nerves coming to this hospital. Last I checked, phones still work."

"Come sit down," Aaliyah insisted. "I get it, you're worried about Desmond. You should've told me the two of you were involved."

"Why...so you could've ran off and told Amir?"

"Justina, you're my best friend. Amir is my

friend too but my loyalty is to you."

"I'm sorry." Justina put her head down. "Seeing Desmond get shot and the blood everywhere really messed me up. I knew I loved him but when I thought I loss him for good, I realized just how much."

"It's okay." Aaliyah said hugging her friend.

"I really am sorry. I shouldn't have said what I did to you and Amir."

Aaliyah took Justina's hand and held them in hers. "Look at me."

Justina lifted up her head and the two women were staring directly in each other's eyes. "What is it?"

"I don't think I ever really apologized for what Amir and I did to you."

"Aaliyah, you don't..."

"Let me finish," Aaliyah said, cutting Justina off. "We were all so young back then and I'll admit, I was a lot more self centered. I don't think I knew or even cared how much we hurt you. Then when everything happened with your mother, I used that as an excuse to dismiss the pain we caused. What we did was wrong and I'm sorry. I hope you can find it in your heart to forgive me."

"Aaliyah, I waited so long to hear you say

those words to me. If only…" Justina's words faded.

"If only what?"

If only you had said this years ago, it could've prevented so much damage I caused. I wouldn't have become a heartless killer who teamed up with Maya to bring you down, Justina thought to herself.

"If only we could turn back time but we can't," Justina said full of contrite. "We both made mistakes, so yes I accept your apology and I hope you can forgive me too."

"I already have," Aaliyah beamed. The two best friends embraced. They say forgiveness means letting go of the past but it was already written, it would define Aaliyah and Justina's future.

Chapter Five

Broken People

"Fuck!" Dale roared punching his fist through the glass mirror.

"Man, what you doing!" his friend Owen yelled. "Damn, your hand is bleeding."

"Who gives a fuck," Dale scoffed.

"Nigga, I do," Owen said, turning on the cold water. "Put yo' hand under there."

Dale reluctantly did so. As the water washed

the blood down the drain, he couldn't help but stare at his reflection. He wasn't sure he recognized the man in the mirror.

I can't believe I shot Desmond. If he dies, I'll never forgive myself. That's my people and I let my emotions get the best of me, Dale thought to himself as he had flashbacks to what happened earlier that day. When he woke up the morning of his wedding, Dale had every intention of taking out Aaliyah's entire family. He wanted her to feel the same betrayal and pain he did, after waking up from his coma and remembering what Nesa told him. He had meticulously planned their execution and made sure his army of men were well prepared. All was going smoothly until Desmond stepped in. He respected him as a longtime friend and business associate. He convinced him that murder wasn't the way to exact revenge against the people he held responsible for his brother's death.

Dale was ready to put down his gun but when he locked eyes with Supreme, his fury erupted all over again. Now, his inability to control his rage might cost Dale everything.

"Any news on Desmond?" Dale asked as he wrapped a towel around the cut on his hand.

"Nah, not yet. I placed some calls but it's hard getting information over the phone. I have somebody at the hospital he was taken to, trying to get answers."

"Man, if Desmond don't make it..." Dale closed his eyes.

"Don't even think that shit. Desmond like us...he a soldier. He gon' pull through," Owen said confidently.

"But he should've never took that bullet in the first place. I really fucked up."

"No! I ain't gon' let you stand here and blame yourself. This shit 'bout Emory...your brother. That nigga was like a brother to me too. He dead and gone! Where's the justice in that?"

"But look at me now," Dale said walking out the bathroom. "Emory still dead, Desmond in the hospital fighting for his life and I'm sure the police are hunting me down as we speak."

"We already considered that, which is why we got this crib for you to hide out at until we decided your next move," Owen reminded him.

"I know but none of this shit is working out like we planned," Dale said shaking his head.

"We can still kill Supreme and the rest of Aaliyah's family, if that's what you want to do.

Everybody standing by waiting for you to give the order. Just tell me what you wanna do," Owen stated.

"I wanna bring my brother home but I can't," Dale said staring out the window. He was in the middle of nowhere with nothing but his thoughts to consume him. "Without my brother, I have no real family left and somebody has to pay for that. Call my men. Let them know it's time to make our next move."

"I really don't think all this security is necessary," Aaliyah said to Nico when she got back to her hotel room.

"Like I told you on our way over here. Either deal with the extra guards or you can stay at my house. Ideally that's what I'd prefer but for whatever reason, you insisted on coming back here," Nico commented while walking through Aaliyah's hotel suite for the third time.

"Dad, nobody is here. You and the two men posted outside already checked at least six times," she huffed kicking off her heels.

"After what happened earlier today, I'm not

taking any chances."

"Don't you mean what happened at my wedding. You keep referring to it like this was some random act and it wasn't. The man I was supposed to spend the rest of my life with, turned on me and my family. Instead of being on my honeymoon, I'm here all alone."

"Aaliyah, you're not alone," Nico said, sitting down next to his daughter on the edge of the bed. "I know you don't want to hear it but this is the best thing that could've happened to you."

"Excuse me!"

"What if you and Dale did get married today, started a family and then he found out Supreme killed his brother. It wouldn't be so easy to walk away once kids are involved. I know it's difficult to mend a broken heart but it's a lot easier as a single woman than a married one with kids."

"Thanks for the fatherly advice but I really want to be alone right now," Aaliyah sighed, standing up.

"Just know, I love you baby girl and if you need anything, call me." Nico kissed Aaliyah on her forehead before leaving.

Once her father was gone, Aaliyah reached for her cell phone. She kept hoping there would be a missed call from Dale or even a text message but there was nothing.

I know I should hate Dale but I love him now as much as I did before. What we have is worth fighting for and I refuse to give up on our love, Aaliyah thought to herself while standing in the middle of the hotel room in her wedding dress, as tears streamed down her face.

Like everyone else who was an avid social media user, Taren heard about the shooting at Aaliyah's wedding. When it was reported Supreme had been taken to the hospital, going off a hunch, Taren decided to stake out the same hospital Angel was taken to recover after the club explosion. She sat in her rental car waiting patiently to see if Angel would make an appearance. By the time she arrived, Taren missed Aaliyah and Angel coming in but to her surprise and delight she caught Dominique exiting the hospital with Clarissa.

"I should run that bitch over right now," Taren said out loud as she eyed the women who seemed to be having an intense conversation.

Taren began to put her foot on the gas, thinking how easy it would be to erase Dominique and her friend, if she got in the way. Without Dominique around, there would be no one left to identify her as the person who killed Aspen and caused the explosion at Diamonds & Pearls strip club. She was prepared to make her move until a knock on the window snapped Taren out of her scheming.

"Roll down your window!" the police officer ordered sounding irate, which he was. This was his third time trying to get Taren's attention. Between her music being on full blast and focusing on Dominique, Taren was in her own world and hadn't noticed he was standing there.

"Is there a problem, officer?" Taren asked politely turning down the radio.

"You don't see the sign in front of you?" he pointed his finger up. "It says no parking. That means you need to move your vehicle now."

"I'm so sorry. I was waiting for my aunt to come out."

"Don't be sorry, just move your car!" he barked.

Taren rolled her window back up and realized the officer wasn't going to move until she did what he asked. She gave him a slight smile and drove off. For a brief second Taren glanced over at Dominque as she drove by. From the rear-view mirror, she could see the annoying officer was still clocking her. She waited until she was completely out of sight to turn around. Taren wasn't able to kill Dominique then but now that she located her former prisoner, she was on her radar. There was only one way to exit the hospital parking lot, so Taren parked across the street and waited patiently for Clarissa and Dominique to leave.

"You got lucky this time but now I got yo' ass and I ain't letting you get away again," Taren promised, as she pulled behind Clarissa's SUV.

"Are you sure you don't want me to stay here with you? I know Aaliyah would understand if I couldn't come see her until later," Precious said to Supreme as he was getting out the shower.

"I'm positive. I appreciate you being so attentive but I'm fine. The bullet only grazed me. Trust me, Aaliyah is in much more pain than I am. Go be with our daughter. I wish I could come with you."

"Then, why don't you?"

"Nico and Amir are stopping by."

"What?! Why are they coming here?"

"Amir didn't go into details on the phone but it has something to do with Genesis," Supreme explained.

"It must be serious if Nico is tagging along and you're not complaining about it," Precious remarked.

"Genesis is my man and if he needs my help, then I have no problem putting my dislike for Nico aside."

"That's sweet," Precious smiled, giving Supreme a kiss. "So, you know, Nico knows we got remarried," she winked. "It slipped out but I'll tell you about it later. Right now, let me go see Aaliyah. Call me if you need me!" Precious gave Supreme an air kiss before heading out.

Supreme hurried and got dressed, knowing Amir and Nico would be there shortly. "Fuck!" he grumbled when putting on his shirt. He didn't want Precious to worry but Supreme was in a lot of pain from where the bullet hit his shoulder. But he had no time to get caught up in his discomfort. Supreme was too consumed with worrying about Aaliyah. He felt responsible for ruining her wedding and her relationship with Dale. Now he was concerned about Genesis and he needed to speak with T-Roc. Supreme wanted to know if the cops had any leads on who murdered Delondo and his wife.

"Coming!" Supreme shouted when he heard a knock, quickly shifting his thoughts from T-Roc to opening the door. "Come on in," he told Amir and Nico.

"Thanks for letting us stop by on such short notice," Amir said sitting down.

"No problem. From the tone of your voice on the phone, I'm assuming this is serious."

"It is," Nico jumped in and said. "Is Precious here?"

"No. She went to see Aaliyah. Why you ask?" Supreme wanted to know.

"What we're about to discuss, we want as few people as possible to know about it," Nico made clear.

"As you know Precious is my wife, so I'll decide what she should and shouldn't know," Supreme shot back.

"I had no idea you and Precious remarried. Congrats!" Amir stood up and shook Supreme's hand.

"Thank you, Amir...no congrats from you, Nico?" Supreme grinned.

"I have to get to the airport soon, so let me fill you in on what's going on," Amir said, noticing the frown on Nico's face. He was working on limited time and didn't need their discussion to be delayed due to Nico and Supreme exchanging slick jabs with each other.

"You have my full attention." Supreme folded his arms and sat on the armrest of the couch, listening intently.

"I got a call from Arnez right before the wedding started," Amir revealed.

"Damn!" Supreme grunted. "So, it's true," he shook his head.

"You knew Arnez was alive?" Nico questioned in an accusatory tone.

"I got word there was a possibility and I had my men investigating."

"Why in the hell didn't you say something?!" Nico barked.

"Because for the first time in a very long time, Genesis seemed happy. I didn't want to disrupt that happiness until I knew this wasn't some street rumor but the real deal."

"You should've said something!" Nico continued. "We could've prevented this shit."

"Hold on," Amir put his hand up. "This isn't Supreme's fault. Even if we knew there was a chance Arnez was alive, none of us could've predicted his next move."

"What has Arnez done now?" Supreme wanted to know.

"He kidnapped Skylar and Genevieve," Amir told Supreme.

"What! This guy," Supreme sighed. "I guess Arnez has no idea Genevieve isn't Genesis's daughter."

"She is his daughter," Nico stated.

"No. I spoke to Genesis before he left the country. He was devastated. He told me the paternity test revealed Genevieve wasn't his." Supreme noticed Nico shooting Amir a quick glare and he had his head down. "Does one of you want to tell me what's going on?"

"I think it should be Amir," Nico nodded.

"I messed up," Amir finally said.

"Don't sugarcoat that shit. You more than messed up," Nico griped. "You did it. You need to own up to that fucked up bullshit."

"I paid to have the test switched," Amir admitted, full of shame.

Supreme let out a deep sigh. "There's nothing I can say to make you feel worse then you already do. Let's focus on bringing your sister home."

"I'm not surprised you're being so easy on Amir. You can relate since you have your own history of switching paternity tests." Nico had been waiting to take that stab at Supreme.

"I'ma ignore your petty comment because we have more pressing issues, like finding Skylar and Genevieve. Amir, what does Genesis want us to do?" Supreme asked.

"He's on his way back to New York. I'm leaving today and Nico is flying back on Tuesday. My dad wants all of us to get together, so we can devise a plan. If you can get back to New York as soon as possible, that would be great."

"Precious can stay here with Aaliyah and I can leave tomorrow."

"I know my dad will appreciate that, Supreme."

"This Arnez situation has gone on long enough. It's time for us to get rid of that devil for good this time."

"I agree," Nico added.

"If there isn't anything else, I'ma head out

and go see Aaliyah, especially since I need to cut my trip short."

"No, we're good. I'll see you tomorrow then," Amir nodded.

"For sure," Supreme nodded back. "Always a pleasure, Nico," he called out as he was walking out door. Supreme let out a light chuckle.

To say Nico and Supreme loathed one another would be an understatement. Their love for Aaliyah was the only thing that bonded them. But even with their mutual detest, when necessary, they were able to put their differences aside for the greater good. And although neither would ever admit it, they also found amusement in getting under each other's skin.

Chapter Six

Torn

"That's the entire story from beginning to end," Angel said feeling exhausted after giving Darien a detailed account of everything that transpired at Aaliyah's wedding.

"Babe, that sound like some shit out a movie. It's a miracle no one ended up dead. How's Aaliyah holding up?"

"Decent under the circumstances but it's

going to take a long time for her to get over this, if she ever does. Dale ruined what was supposed to be a magical day. What makes matters worse is she's still in love with hm."

"That's not surprising but with love and support from her family, she'll get through it."

"I agree. I know I'm supposed to come see you this weekend but if you don't mind, I really want to stay here a little longer and be with my sister."

"Of course. I know Aaliyah needs you right now," Darien said.

"Thanks for being so understanding."

"That's what a husband is supposed to be."

"Yeah, but a lot of them aren't. I feel lucky to have you and I can't wait to be with my amazing husband again because I miss you like crazy."

"We just have to keep facetiming each other until you get here."

"I'll be there sooner than you think and I'm going to show you how much you've been missed."

"Promise."

"Yes...Darien let me call you back," Angel blurted suddenly.

"Is something wrong...are you okay?"

"I'm fine. I love you and I'll call you later on." Angel blew her husband a kiss goodbye and hung up. She then leaped out the bed, scrambling to find the television remote. "There it is!" she exclaimed, turning up the volume.

An unidentified body has been pulled out of Lake Okeechobee which covers 700 square miles. So far, the authorities have given us very limited information, only saying it's the body of a female in her early to late twenties and they're investigating this case as a homicide. We will be following this story closely and will keep you posted.

Angel tossed down the remote after the news cut to a commercial break. Her mouth remained wide open. She was positive hundreds if not thousands of women went missing in Florida but Angel had an eerie feeling this particular body being pulled out the water was Nesa.

"Maybe I'm wrong," Angel wanted to believe, struggling with the idea that Nesa had been murdered. No matter how hard she tried to shake the notion, her gut wouldn't allow it. "I'm letting my overactive imagination get the best of me," she reasoned. Angel decided to put the thought out of her mind, go take a shower and start her day.

"Are you expecting a call?" Precious said as her and Aaliyah were sitting outside having brunch. "I'm only asking because you keep looking at your phone."

"No." Aaliyah shook her head, breaking off a piece of her croissant.

"Let me guess, you're hoping to hear from Dale."

"You must think I'm so dumb."

"Of course not," Precious said reaching over the table and gently touching Aaliyah's hand. "Trust me, I've been there."

Precious thought back to the time Nico shot her while she was pregnant with Supreme's baby. She survived but their unborn child didn't. Even after something so horrific, for a brief time when she believed Supreme was dead, she reconciled with Nico.

"You? I can't even imagine. You're like the strongest woman I know."

"Even strong women have weaknesses."

"Who was your weakness?"

"At one time or another, Nico and Supreme,"

Precious laughed.

"Well Dale is my weakness. I want him back. I know I shouldn't but I do. But you know what's more devastating than anything."

"What?"

"He doesn't want me." Aaliyah teared up.

"I hate seeing you in so much pain. You're still my baby girl. I wish I could erase it all away but I can't. It's a journey every woman in love has to take. Only you know how far you're willing to go."

"I wanna go all the way," Aaliyah admitted. "I can't imagine my life without Dale in it."

"I understand but one person can't make a relationship work. Whether justified or not, Dale hates Supreme for killing his brother and feels betrayed by you for not telling him. Those are some serious obstacles to get through. In your heart, do you believe Dale could ever move past that and forgive you?"

"I think he will once he knows I'm carrying his child."

"Aaliyah, you're pregnant?!" Precious put her hand over her mouth completely stunned. "My baby is having a baby," her voice quivered. She went over to Aaliyah and embraced her tightly.

"Mom, I want Dale back. I want us to be a family," Aaliyah cried.

"Then you'll have him. We'll make it happen. I promise."

"What's going on out here?" Supreme asked, walking out on the balcony startling Precious and Aaliyah. Precious quickly stood up while Aaliyah wiped her tears away not wanting her dad to see her crying.

"Supreme, what are you doing here? I thought you were meeting with Amir and Nico."

"I did meet with them. The situation with Genesis is much more serious than I originally thought. I have to go back to New York tomorrow but I wanted to see Aaliyah before I left. How is my beautiful daughter?" Supreme sat down in the chair next to Aaliyah.

"I'm fine, daddy."

"You don't have to lie to me."

"How is your shoulder? Is it healing okay?" Aaliyah asked trying to divert the conversation away from her.

"I'm fine. I'm more concerned about you. I don't want you to be afraid."

"What do you mean afraid?" Aaliyah looked at her dad with confusion.

"That Dale is going to come back and harm you in some way. I have my men on it. They are looking for him as we speak. I promise he will be dealt with."

"You can't do that!" Aaliyah uttered. "I don't want you to kill Dale."

"Supreme, can I speak with you inside?"

"In a minute. Let me finish talking to Aaliyah. Baby girl, I get you're emotional right now but Dale wanted to kill not only me but your entire family. You know he has to go."

"Supreme, I need to talk to you now!" Precious put emphasis on the word now, letting Supreme know this wasn't up for debate.

"Let me go speak with your mother and when I get back we can finish our talk." Supreme kissed Aaliyah on her forehead before following Precious inside. "What's so important you couldn't wait until I finished talking to Aaliyah?" he asked.

Precious didn't respond until after she closed the balcony door. "You need to back off on the Dale conversation. Aaliyah isn't ready. It won't end well," Precious warned.

"Where is this coming from? Aaliyah is hurt which is understandable but when she calms down, she'll realize Dale needs to be out of her life permanently," Supreme stated with confidence.

"Aaliyah wants him back, Supreme. She told me so right before you walked in."

"It doesn't matter because it's not gonna happen," he said dismissively. "Dale tried to kill me and he would've killed you too and everyone else Aaliyah loved if Desmond hadn't taken the bullet. We have no choice but to take him out before he comes at us again because he will."

"Not necessarily." Precious glided her index finger across her lip as if in deep thought.

"Normally you're the first person ready to seek retribution for anyone who comes after our family. What's the hesitation now?"

"Aaliyah is pregnant with Dale's child. That trumps everything."

"I'm assuming Dale doesn't know...damn," Supreme seethed.

"You know this changes everything. We can't kill Dale. As a matter of fact, Aaliyah wants to reconcile with him."

"She what!" Supreme yelled.

"Keep your voice down!" Precious fumed. "I know this isn't what you want to hear. What Dale did at that wedding was reprehensible but if Aaliyah wants to forgive him, then we have to support her decision."

"No, we don't," Supreme refuted. "I'm not gonna give Dale another opportunity to harm this family."

"This isn't negotiable, Supreme. I'm not gonna risk alienating my daughter and possibly my grandchild over your need to pursue immediate revenge against Dale."

"So, what do you expect for me to do, Precious?" he asked becoming incensed.

"Give Aaliyah time to work things out with Dale."

"You are actually considering letting the two of them be together? Do you know how crazy that is! You saw what Dale is capable of. You want Aaliyah to be married to a man like that?"

"Aaliyah and the baby she's carrying, is my only concern right now. We have a much better chance of protecting them both, if she feels we're on her side."

"Fine, I'll back off killing Dale but I hope we both don't live to regret it."

Supreme walked off and went back outside to finish his conversation with Aaliyah, leaving Precious to contemplate if she was making the right decision. Supreme was right, at the moment, Dale was a threat to all of them but Aaliyah didn't see it that way. Precious knew her daughter and as long as she believed there was a chance her and Dale could reunite, she would rebel against them if it meant protecting him. Precious wasn't willing to risk losing Aaliyah but she also had to make sure Dale wasn't allowed to cause any more damage.

Chapter Seven

Down For Whatever

"It feels so good to wake up in my own bed, with you next to me," Desmond said to Justina.

"I feel the exact same way." Justina leaned over and kissed Desmond. "But remember, the doctor said you have to take it easy for the next couple weeks."

"I don't plan to go back to the club until next week. For now, I'll be working from home."

"Good and I'll be right here keeping an eye on you," Justina winked.

"I wouldn't want it any other way. I like having you here with me. Now that everyone knows about us, I think we should make it permanent."

"What are you saying?"

"You already agreed to stay here for the next couple weeks and nurse me back to health, why do you have to leave? We can live together."

"Desmond, I don't know about that," Justina said, resistant to the idea. "The only man I've ever lived with is my father."

"I'll tell you what. Let's see how things go the next couple weeks and then decide. I don't want you to feel pressured."

"Okay we can do that," Justina smiled. "Now let me go make you some breakfast because you can't take your medicine on an empty stomach," she giggled, playfully hitting Desmond with the pillow.

"Don't burn down the house while you in there tryna cook!" Desmond joked as Justina headed downstairs. "Babe!" he called out when he heard her cell ringing but she was already gone. When he reached over to get her phone off the nightstand, Desmond accidentally knocked over her purse. "Damn," he huffed getting out of bed.

"She got a lot of damn shit in here," Desmond commented while picking up all the items that fell on the floor. "What the hell!" he exclaimed, when one thing in particular caught his eye.

"Babe, I forgot to ask how you like your eggs, scrambled or..." Justina stopped in her tracks when she saw what Desmond was holding in his hand.

"You pregnant?" he asked holding up a pregnancy test. "Don't lie to me, Justina." Desmond stated before she even opened her mouth to respond.

"Yes. I mean the first two pregnancy tests I took came back positive. That's my third one. I guess I keep hoping the result will be different."

"Why because you don't want to have my baby?"

"That's not the reason at all."

"Then what?"

"I don't know if it's yours. The baby could be Amir's," Justina confessed.

"Did you plan on telling me about the pregnancy?" Desmond wanted to know.

"Honestly, I'm not sure. I was debating

whether I should even go through with the pregnancy."

"You're gonna have an abortion?" Desmond's eyes filled with discontent.

"What choice do I really have? If I have this baby and it turns out you're not the father, I can guarantee you, Amir will want joint custody. I'll be connected to him forever and I don't think our relationship can survive that."

Desmond stood up and sat down on the bed. He let what Justina said sink in. "I'ma ask you a question and I want you to tell me the truth."

"I'm so past lying to you, Desmond. You know my darkest secrets. If I can tell anyone the truth, it's you," Justina said.

"Do you still love Amir...be honest?"

"No! I swear on everything. I don't love Amir. You're the only man I love."

"Do you want us to be together? I mean fo-real. Not no bullshit relationship but a real commitment where you know I have your back and you have mine?"

"I want that more than anything. You're the first man I've ever even thought it was possible to share a connection like that with. That's why when I found out I was pregnant, I got scared.

Seeing you get shot, my heart dropped and then I thought you might die. When you survived, I found myself thinking I might lose you anyway if this baby wasn't yours."

"Is that why you resisted when I asked you to move in with me?"

Justina nodded her head. "I hadn't decided what I was going to do about this pregnancy. I felt it would be a mistake for us to live together if I wanted to keep the baby, especially if you're not the father."

"Come sit down," Desmond said patting a spot next to him in the bed. "After I got shot but before I lost consciousness, you were the last thought in my head. It was your face I wanted to see again," he divulged to Justina while holding her hand. "I love you and I want to spend the rest of my life with you, whether the baby you're carrying is mine or not."

"You mean that?" Justina's eyes watered up.

"Without a doubt. That baby is a part of you. How could I not love it?"

"What about Amir? If he's the father, he's going to fight me for custody. I can feel it."

"Not if we're married before the baby is born. Then legally, it's our baby."

"You're saying you want to get married?"

"Yes. We can have something very small. Then later on, we can plan a huge wedding."

"I don't need a big wedding or any of that hoopla. I just need you." Justina kissed Desmond passionately.

"Does that mean yes you'll marry me?"

"Yes! Yes! Yes! I'll marry you Desmond Blackwell!"

"Thank you so much for coming by," Aaliyah beamed when she let Angel in. "You look so pretty. I love your outfit," she commented on the lavender, wide leg, sleeveless jumpsuit.

"Thanks, and I'm glad you asked me to stop by. I wanted to come spend time with my sister and of course I brought your favorites from Starbucks," Angel smiled.

"How lucky am I to have you," Aaliyah said taking her drink and caramelized apple pound cake. "I needed this."

"Well, I know you're still not ready to go out, so I figured I would bring the goodies to you."

"And it's much appreciated. Let's go sit

72

outside on the balcony. I guess it's my way of not feeling completely shut off from the world."

"What happened at your wedding is still fresh. Take as much time as you need, there's no rush."

"It's been three weeks, Angel. I can't stay hidden in my hotel suite forever. I even had to turn my comments off on my Instagram page. People have been speculating about what happened at my wedding and why I didn't get married. I couldn't take it anymore."

"That's why I don't do social media. The scrutiny will drive you crazy. I know you enjoy it and I'm not telling you to stop. But you can't let it dictate your life. Besides your family, you don't owe anyone an explanation, unless that's what you want to do."

"True but when you share every aspect of your life on social media, you can't really blame people when they want answers. Honestly, I wanna give it to them but what do I say...the love of my life hates me and wanted to kill my entire family because my dad murdered his brother and I kept the truth from him." Aaliyah rolled her eyes. "Boy, they probably wouldn't believe me even if I told them."

"Yeah, I think you should keep that part of the story to yourself. You'll definitely have the police knocking at your door," Angel laughed.

"Didn't I tell you, they've already been here," Aaliyah shrugged, taking a sip of her drink.

"No, you didn't. What did they say?"

"Supreme had one of his high-priced lawyers here with me so they kept it cute. I stuck to my story, it was really chaotic and I didn't see who shot Desmond. Luckily, Desmond is also telling the same story. No one who attended the wedding is cooperating with the police so they've basically hit a dead end."

"How does Supreme feel about you protecting Dale? Especially since the man did try to kill him."

"He's been surprisingly very understanding. Probably because my mother told him about the pregnancy."

"Have you told Dale about the baby yet?"

"No, only because I haven't had the chance. He hasn't contacted me and I tried calling him but he disconnected his phone. It may sound crazy but I'm excited about the baby. Knowing a part of us is growing inside of me makes me feel connected to Dale, even if I have no idea where he is."

"Aaliyah, please don't take this the wrong way but you're not even a little worried, about wanting to be with a man, who plotted to take out your family at your wedding?" Angel wondered.

"If I grew up in a regular, traditional family, I probably would be worried," Aaliyah smirked. "Not sure if our father filled you in but we are a notorious bunch. I knew Dale was no saint. I don't think I could've fell in love with him, if we weren't cut from the same cloth. People in my circle aren't good like you, Angel. We are all seriously flawed. So, although I don't like what Dale did, I do understand and I forgive him."

"I'm not a saint either, Aaliyah and trust me, I have a lot of flaws."

"That might be true but you give to others without wanting anything in return. I've seen it with my own eyes. Your name fits you perfectly because you are an angel. I on the other hand can be extremely selfish and admittedly, I'm a spoiled brat. But when I fall in love, I love with all my heart. Right or wrong, Dale has my heart and I believe deep down inside, if he can get past his anger, he'll admit I have his heart too."

"Wake up! Wake up!" Owen roared, storming into Dale's bedroom.

"Man, what is it?" Dale mumbled, fighting to come out his sleep.

"Yo, get the fuck up! There's a fleet of SUV's out front. The house is surrounded with men and all of them are strapped."

"The feds the police?!" Dale flung the comforter off the bed and jumped up reaching for his weapon.

"Did you not hear what I said. We're surrounded. That gun you have in your hand and every weapon in this house ain't gon' do shit to all that gun power outside. We fucked!" Owen barked.

"We out here in the middle of nowhere. How in the hell did they find us?" Dale shook his head as he threw on some sweats and a t-shirt.

"What you wanna do? I can call for backup but by the time they get here, it'll be too late."

"We should've left when we had the chance. Game over now."

"Where you going?" Owen questioned, following behind Dale.

"To open the front door."

"Man, I ain't tryna die or go to jail. Don't answer that door."

"Owen, you didn't shoot nobody, I did. You good. Stay upstairs. I got this."

"Nah, you my boy. Where you go I follow. We in this together," Owen stated, standing right next to Dale when he opened the door.

Just like Owen said, there was half a dozen black tinted SUV's lined up in a single row. There were men dressed in camouflage clothing positioned around the perimeter of the house, all holding semiautomatic rifles legally modified to fire like automatic weapons. None of that shocked Dale as he'd already prepared himself to be greeted with heavy arsenal. What he wasn't prepared for was who stepped out the first SUV.

"Dale, we have a lot to discuss," Precious said, with her own weapon in tow.

Aaliyah's mother was the last person Dale expected to roll up on him. He wasn't sure if he preferred being taken out by the police or a woman he had planned to kill. At this point, it didn't matter. Dale was down for whatever.

Chapter Eight

Warnings

"Aaliyah, this is such an unexpected, pleasant surprise! Give me a hug beautiful!" Justina and Aaliyah stood in the foyer for a long embrace.

"I've missed you so much! And since it's been impossible to get you to stop by the hotel and I'm tired of just talking to you on the phone, I had to come over and see my best friend."

"I'm sorry, babe. I've had so much going on

and Desmond requires a lot of attention," Justina laughed. "But he just left not too long ago, so perfect timing. We have the house to ourselves."

"Is that a wedding ring!" Aaliyah gasped, grabbing Justina's hand.

"Yes! I planned on telling you but like I said it's been crazy over here," Justina said, trying not to sound as nervous as she felt.

"I didn't know things were so serious between you and Desmond. And why didn't you invite me to the wedding? I'm your best friend." Justina could see the hurt on Aaliyah's face. This is what she was trying to avoid. Justina wasn't ready for the twenty-one questions she knew Aaliyah would throw at her.

"I wanted to tell you but..."

"You don't have to say it. I already know why you didn't invite me," Aaliyah said cutting Justina off.

Justina froze as if she believed all her secrets were about to be exposed. "What do mean?"

"You thought I wouldn't be able to handle it because my wedding turned out to be a bust."

"Aaliyah, that's not it at all."

"I'm a big girl. You don't have to worry about hurting my feelings."

"It was really a spare of the moment decision. We had a small wedding right here at the house, my parents weren't even invited. We are going to have a bigger celebration inviting our family and close friends in the future. Of course, I want you right by my side. So, do you forgive me?"

"You don't even have to ask," Aaliyah smiled. The ladies interlocked their arms walking into the living room. "Desmond, has a really beautiful house. The club business must be very profitable," she said after they sat down.

"My husband is doing well for himself."

"I bet you love saying that," Aaliyah cracked.

"I do...I do. How rude of me, can I get you something to drink? We have a full bottle of peach moscato which I know you love."

"No, I'm good. I'm surprised you still have a full bottle left. We both know what a lush you are," Aaliyah joked.

"Yes, I do love me some wine but I've been cutting back...all the way back."

"Is there a reason why?" Aaliyah gave her a peculiar look.

From the second Aaliyah showed up unex- pectedly and noticed Justina's wedding ring, she began debating if she should come clean about the pregnancy. Part of her wanted to keep it a secret a little longer but then Justina figured if she told her now, it would keep Aaliyah from being suspicious in the future.

"I just found out recently I'm pregnant. Desmond is thrilled of course and so am I!" Justina beamed, making sure she made it clear Desmond was the father of the child she's carrying.

"Oh wow! It has been busy over here. How far along are you?"

"Only five weeks," Justina lied. "I had to go to the doctor for a routine checkup last week. Of course, I gave a urine sample and boom the doctor tells me I'm pregnant and how far along I was."

"Marriage and a baby...congrats! I guess this is the perfect time for me to share my news with you too."

"What news?"

"I'm actually three and a half months pregnant."

"OMG! Aaliyah, that's wonderful...right?"

"I mean it isn't exactly how I wanted it to be but I do love this baby growing inside of me," Aaliyah said putting her hand on her stomach.

"You should be. A baby is a blessing. How long have you known?"

"I found out right before I was supposed to

get married. I was so busy planning the perfect wedding that I hadn't even noticed I was late, like really late."

"I'm guessing you didn't have a chance to tell Dale before the wedding because he would've never done what he did, if he knew you were carrying his baby."

"Justina, thank you for saying that. I feel like my family is looking at Dale like he is some monster and I'm crazy for wanting to be with him after what he did."

"You're not crazy. I know how much Dale loved you and I'm sure he still does. Once he finds out you're carrying his child, Dale's going to wish he can take it all back."

"You know what I wish?"

"What?"

"I wish I knew how he found out in the first place. I didn't even know until Amir told me. It all happened when Maya and Arnez were holding me hostage and my father was trying to find me before I ended up dead. Somebody had to tell Dale but who is the question."

Justina didn't know how to respond to what Aaliyah said. For the first time, she was consumed with guilt. Justina was responsible for ruining her wedding and she prayed Aaliyah would never find out.

"I hope everything works out for you, Dale and the baby your carrying," was all Justina could manage to say.

"Turn the volume up," Aaliyah said. She was so fixated on the television screen that she hadn't even heard what Justina said. "I've been following this story."

"Sure." Justina's heart started racing when she saw Nesa's face on the screen.

"That woman looks so familiar to me for some reason," Aaliyah commented, fully intrigued with what the newscaster was reporting. "She doesn't look familiar to you?"

"No, I've never seen her before."

"A few weeks ago, they pulled a dead woman out some lake. They've finally been able to put a name to the body. How awful it must be for her family, knowing she was tossed in the water like a piece of trash. She must've have really pissed off the wrong person...so sad," Aaliyah sighed.

"Sad indeed. Let's watch something else," Justina said turning the channel. "This is way too depressing."

"You're right. We should be celebrating.

Both of us are pregnant at the same time. How crazy but wonderful is that. Our kids will grow up together being best friends just like us. OMG wouldn't it be cool if we both had girls?"

"That would be pretty neat. Are you sure you don't want anything to drink? I'm super thirsty."

"I guess I'll have some juice," Aaliyah said.

"Cool, I'll be back shortly." Justina wasn't sure if it was pregnancy hormones running rampant or if she had developed a conscious but she had to get out of that room. Knowing she was solely responsible for Dale learning the truth and turning on Aaliyah and then seeing Nesa's face splashed across her television screen, made her nauseated. When she reached the kitchen, Justina leaned on the marble island and took a deep breath.

I don't know if I should be relieved or scared that Nesa is dead. Desmond said he would handle the situation, does that mean he killed her? If so would the police be able to trace her murder back to him? I can't lose Desmond. Justina thought to herself, ready to cry. *Fuck! Get it together Justina. This isn't the time for you to turn into a weak, emotional wreck. You have a husband and an unborn baby to protect by any means necessary.*

Justina took another deep breath but this time it was to put her game face back on. Aaliyah was no dummy and Justina knew if she wanted to keep her best friend in the dark about all of her shenanigans, then she had to remain on point.

"Are having all these men in here with guns pointed in my direction really necessary?" Dale asked Precious, as she stared him down from across the room.

"Under the circumstances, I think it's best to take precautions."

"Clearly, you came here to kill me for what I did to Aaliyah and Supreme. Why haven't you just gotten it over with? Or are you going to take some sort of pleasure in torturing me?"

"Dale, I don't have any of intentions of killing you...yet." Precious walked towards Dale and took a seat in the chair directly across from him. "Believe it or not, I can empathize with you. Family is the most important thing in the world, so losing your only brother had to be devastating. So, imagine how frightened all of us felt when we believed Aaliyah might be dead."

"I was just as scared too. At that time Aaliyah was my world and Emory knew it. Ya' can try to spit on his name 'cause he dead and ain't here to defend himself but you'll never make me believe my brother knew anything about Aaliyah's kidnapping." Dale was adamant in his belief and defending his brother.

"I knew you would say that so I came with receipts." Precious had two envelopes in her hand. She slid one across the table to Dale.

"What's this?" Dale asked picking it up.

"Open it. Unless you're afraid of the truth."

"I ain't afraid of shit," Dale said ripping open the envelope and looking over the papers.

"Supreme didn't want to turn this information over to me because of course he doesn't want Aaliyah to have anything to do with you. He prefers you being dead. But I wanted you to have all the facts before the final decision was made, if you were going to live or die," Precious stated.

"Cut the bullshit. I know you have no intention of letting me live," Dale shrugged, continuing to look over the papers. "This doesn't mean anything," Dale disputed, tossing the papers down.

"Those are text messages that were exchanged between your brother, Arnez and Maya, discussing what should be done with Aaliyah. If you look at the dates, it's clearly during the time when my daughter was missing."

"These could be fake. Supreme could've easily had them altered," Dale retorted.

"If this doesn't convince you then you're determined to stay in denial." Precious slid Dale the other envelope.

Dale's eyes widened as he scanned each picture. Some were with Emory and Arnez but most were with his brother and Maya. It was obvious from the photos Emory and Maya's relationship was personal.

"Maybe your brother didn't know all the details but he knew enough to come to you and save Aaliyah. Instead my daughter could've died and me too. But you know who did end up dead, my father. If Emory would've told you about Maya's involvement, we could've took her down and she would've never had the chance to murder my dad. And you know how much Aaliyah loved and admired her grandfather."

Dale read through the text messages again and then stared at the photos. "Why would Emory do this to me," he mumbled as he faced the truth. "I know my brother had his ways but I never thought he would betray me...not like this." Dale balled up his fist and pounded them down on the table. "I really fucked up."

"Yeah you did," Precious agreed.

"I'm sure Aaliyah hates me. I guess you wanted me to know the truth and feel like shit before you killed me. Well, it worked," Dale shook his head. "Can you do me one favor?"

"What's that?" Precious asked.

"Can you tell Aaliyah I'm sorry for ruining our wedding and that I love her."

"Nope, I can't do that. But you can tell Aaliyah yourself."

"Excuse me?"

"I'm not gonna kill you, Dale."

"Why not?"

"Because my daughter doesn't hate you. Aaliyah believes you're the love of her life and she's carrying your baby. I can't allow anyone to kill the father of her child."

"Aaliyah is pregnant," Dale repeated, making sure what he heard was true. "I'm gonna be a father." He put his head down becoming emotional.

"Yes, you are. I threw you a lifeline because I love my daughter more than anything. But Dale, if you don't treat Aaliyah and my grandchild right, I will personally kill you. I promise," Precious warned.

Chapter Nine

Dreams Destroyed

"Mr. Blackwell, it is such a pleasure to see you," Mrs. Armstrong smiled when she let Desmond in.

"Desmond! You're here!" Dominique ran up and gave him a hug. "I was hoping you would come see us soon."

"Between recuperating, working from home and finally going back to the club, I've been juggling a lot. But I wanted to personally come over and check up on you."

"I'm doing really good and even better now that you're here. Come sit down. Can I get you anything?" Dominique offered, taking Desmond's hand leading him to the couch.

"I'll take a bottle water if you have any."

"I do. I'll be right back." Dominique skipped away in bliss. Her infatuation with Desmond hadn't faded a bit.

"I think you should bring down the flirting just a notch," Mrs. Armstrong stopped Dominique in the hallway and said.

"You're the one who told me what a great catch Desmond was and I would be crazy not to go after what I wanted."

"True but that was before Mr. Blackwell showed up wearing a wedding band. If you weren't so busy flirting with him, maybe you would've noticed," Mrs. Armstrong mocked.

All the color drained from Dominique's face within seconds. "There's no way Desmond got married." Dominique refused to believe it.

"There's only one way to find out. You better ask him," Mrs. Armstrong said walking off.

Dominique went and retrieved a bottle water out the refrigerator and headed back to Desmond. "Here you go."

"Thanks." Desmond took the water with his right hand and because of the way his left hand was positioned, Dominique couldn't see if he was wearing a wedding ring. "How are you really doing? I'm sure you're growing tired of the current situation."

"I would be lying if I didn't say I wanted my old life back. I loved dancing at the club and having the freedom to come and go as I please."

"Like when you came to see me at the hospital?"

"You hadn't mentioned that when we spoke a few times, so I was thinking maybe Justina didn't say anything but I guess I was wrong."

"She did mention it to me." Desmond gave a half smile, laughing to himself at how Justina was practically spitting fire when she told him about her encounter with Dominique.

"I'm not going to apologize for coming to see you. I was worried. I wanted to make sure you were okay. I consider you to be a friend, Desmond."

"I know and I feel the same way about you."

"I'm glad."

"Listen, I want to be honest with you. My men haven't been able to locate Taren yet. It's disappointing but it also makes me extremely angry. The longer she stays under the radar, the more concerned I become we'll never be able to find her."

"Nobody has heard from or seen Taren in months. Maybe she's not coming back," Dominique tried to convince herself. "She knows she's on top of a lot of people's shit list and will more than likely end up dead if she shows her face in Miami. We might've seen the last of Taren."

"You might be right. She suckered Angel out of a lot of money. More than enough to disappear and start her life over somewhere else. Maybe you're not in danger any longer."

"Does that mean I can go back to work?!"

"Are you ready for that?"

"Yes! I've been ready."

"Give me a couple days to work some kinks out. I would only feel comfortable if I had a security detail on you. I wanna make sure I have the right man for the job."

"Thank you for always protecting me. I know I'm safe with you," Dominique smiled. "Desmond, can I ask you a question?"

"Of course."

"Maybe I'm mistaken but I thought I saw a

ring on your finger," she said coyly. "Did you get married?"

"Actually, I did," Desmond conceded putting up his left hand, exposing his platinum wedding band.

Dominique felt like her heart had been ripped out. She convinced herself there was a real chance of them being together as a couple and now her fairytale was being destroyed.

"I'm assuming you married..." Dominique hesitated, unable to bring herself to say Justina's name.

"Yes, I married Justina. We're also expecting a baby."

Dominique wasn't sure how much more heartbreak she could take but she pulled it together, and didn't cry a river like she wanted. "I guess that means you want me to leave here soon," Dominique said looking around the plush condo Desmond had her staying at.

"I told you before and me getting married doesn't change that. You can stay here for as long as you want. I know you haven't been working and you need time to get back on your feet. There's no rush for you to go. I prefer you to stay longer. That way Mrs. Armstrong can continue to monitor things and I know you'll be safe here."

"Are you sure your wife isn't gonna show up and throw me out?"

"I give you my word, Justina will not be a problem for you. The only thing you need to focus on, is getting ready to make your comeback at the club."

"That's what I'll do."

"Wonderful. I need to be going," Desmond said glancing down at his watch. "If you need anything, give me a call. Talk to you later."

Dominique followed Desmond to the door and once he was gone, she knelt down on the floor, leaned back against the wall and cried her heart out. Desmond was everything she ever wanted in a man and now he belonged to someone else. But Dominique still couldn't' let go.

"I want it jet black with a part on the side and a long swoop that kinda covers my eye," Taren explained to the hairstylist.

"So, you going for the old school Aaliyah look."

"Yeah...yeah. Perfect description except it

ain't old school. That Aaliyah hairstyle is a classic, ain't nothing old school about it," Taren winked.

"True. Are you sure you wanna go black? This red color is poppin.'"

"Positive. The red is cute but I want a more low key color. Plus, you can't do the Aaliyah swoop justice without the black hair," Taren laughed.

"Got it. I'll color your hair, braid it up and sew these tracks in."

"Perfect. Don't nothing look more natural than a good sew in weave."

Taren was looking forward to her new do. Since she was extending her stay in Miami she wanted to jazz things up a bit, especially since she planned on going back to work. This time at a strip club outside of Miami. With her new breasts sitting extra perky, Taren was confident the tips would be rolling in although money wasn't her main motivation. With her coins still being intact, Taren had other motives for wanting to broaden her circle.

"What do you think?" the stylist twirled Taren around in her chair so she was facing the large mirror.

"I love it, Kecia! Now all I need is a red lippie to set this joint off," Taren gushed, posing and blowing kisses.

"Nikki, you's a fool." Kecia laughed, calling Taren by the fake name she'd given her. "But it look hella sexy on you. I'm so used to sewing down wigs with closures, I forgot how dope a traditional weave is."

"For sure and you got my leave out so smooth, it's blending with this hair like it's growing out my scalp. You did that. So, glad I found your salon."

"How did you hear about this place?"

"I was at the nail salon and this chick had a really cute hairstyle. I asked her who did it and she told me about you," Taren lied. She really got the info from Aspen. Her hair was always laid and she bragged constantly about Kecia's salon that was located in the cut, in the outskirts of Miami. Back then, Taren didn't wear weaves but she stored the information in her head.

"Happy you came because this came out gorgeous. Turn around so I can get a picture of the front and then the back," Kecia said.

"Sure! I'll be your hair model." Taren was swinging her hair and posturing as if she thought she had turned into Aaliyah herself. After one last pose, Taren gave Kecia a fat tip and strutted out the salon like she wasn't one of Miami's most wanted.

"I know you're headed to Vegas tonight, so I appreciate you having a late lunch with me before leaving," Desmond stated when Angel sat down.

"You know this is one of my favorite restaurants, how could I decline," Angel teased. "Seriously, I'm glad you called. I wanted to see you before I left but I didn't want to put any pressure on you. You've been through a lot to say the least."

"I have but I'm fully recovered and ready to handle business. Since we're partners in Angel's Girls, I wanted to get it on track."

"I think things have been running smoothly, especially under the circumstances. Have you been receiving the weekly reports my assistant has been sending you?"

"I have and they're good but I believe business can be a lot better."

"In what way? I have a very competent person running the everyday operations and I go into the office at least three times a week to stay abreast of any potential problems."

"Elsa is good at her job but I think we could be bringing in a bigger profit."

"How would you suggest we do that? Most of the girls are already overextended."

"I agree. We need to recruit some new women. I know for a while with the murders of a few of our ladies and being under police scrutiny, we weren't bringing on any new hires. It's hurt our bottom line. But enough time has passed where we can move forward," Desmond said.

"I guess hiring a few more girls will be fine," Angel agreed. "I can set up something with Elsa once I get back from Las Vegas in a few weeks."

"No need to wait. I can get started immediately. Maybe I'll have Justina help."

"Justina? I know you all are seeing each other but why do you need to bring her into your business?"

"We're not just seeing each other, we got married," Desmond said lifting up his hand.

"Married!" Angel was about to say something that would surely piss Desmond off but caught herself. He had already made it clear his relationship with Justina was off limits. Since they were business partners, Angel knew mutual respect was imperative. "If you're happy, then I'm happy for you, Desmond."

"Thank you."

"With that being said, I wouldn't feel comfortable having your wife work at Angel's Girls."

"Why not?"

"I don't think mixing business with your personal relationship would be appropriate."

"I will take your concerns into consideration but I can separate the two and so can Justina. She's extremely smart and I believe she could help take our agency to the next level. Also, per our contractual agreement, I have the right to hire my own office manager to oversee daily operations. Justina would be for me what Elsa is to you."

Angel pressed down on her lower lip to stop the tongue lashing she wanted to give Desmond. She then took a sip of her wine to ease her frustration. The idea of having to work with Justina and see her face even once a week made her head hurt. She prayed Justina would feel the same way and decline her husband's offer.

"Have you spoken to Justina about taking the position? It would require a great deal of responsibility and Justina doesn't really strike me as the type who wants to clock in for work," Angel remarked.

"I haven't run it by Justina yet but I'm optimistic she'll accept the position. Now that she'll be living in Miami full time, I'm sure she'll enjoy having something productive to do."

"I see," Angel nodded taking another sip of her wine.

"Angel, I have a great deal of respect for you. I know whatever personal feelings you have towards my wife, you'll put them aside and keep things professional. Remember, this is business."

"Of course, and I wouldn't expect anything less from your wife," Angel smiled, thinking that Darien's suggestion to give up the company she created, might not be such a bad idea after all.

Chapter Ten

Wicked Ways

When Aaliyah heard the knock on her hotel room door, she assumed it was one of the bodyguards posted out front. Seeing Dale's face instead, sent a chill down her spine.

"What are you doing here?" she finally asked. "I mean I'm surprised to see you here."

"I needed to speak with you. Can I come in?"

"Yes...yes...come in," Aaliyah said nervously,

stepping to the side so Dale could get past her. Her two guards were still posted outside the door which made Aaliyah assume they had been expecting Dale. "Who gave you clearance?" she was curious to know.

"Your mother. I asked her not to tell you."

"When did you speak to my mother and how did she get in touch with you?"

"Precious came to see me. Your mother is very resourceful. I see where you get it from."

"My mother can be extremely resourceful, especially when it's something she wants."

"Or when it comes to you. Your mother truly loves you. I can only respect that. It also makes me question if I ever deserved you, Aaliyah."

"Before you say anything else. I have to know. Did you only come back to me for the baby? If my mother came to see you then I'm positive she told you I'm pregnant."

"She did tell me about the baby but it was after I regretted everything I put you and your family through. I was wrong," Dale acknowledged.

"You were ready to kill my entire family at our wedding, what changed?" Aaliyah questioned.

"Learning the truth about my brother. I know you tried to tell me but I didn't want to believe it. Your mother showed me proof I couldn't dispute."

"I do share some of the blame. When I found out, I should've told you but I guess I wasn't confident enough in our love," Aaliyah hated to admit.

"I think that's what bothered me the most. Learning the truth from someone else. It should've come from you. The woman I wanted to spend the rest of my life with."

"You're right. I should've had faith in our love for one another. I'll always regret my decision not to tell you."

"Yeah, you should have but it still doesn't excuse what I put you through. Supreme and Desmond could've died because of me," Dale shook his head. "Not sure if your dad will ever forgive me but my main concern is you. Can we get past this and be together, Aaliyah?"

"I believe we can, especially since we have a little one to consider." Aaliyah looked down at her stomach. It was still flat as a board in her deep cut bodysuit with low waist jeans but it didn't stop her from rubbing her belly.

"I didn't think I could love you anymore than I already did, until I heard Precious say you were carrying my child. The best of both of us is growing inside of you right now." Dale got choked up and so did Aaliyah.

"I'm amazed myself. It didn't become real to me until I went in for my first prenatal checkup."

"I should've been there with you. I'm sorry. But if you let me, I'll never miss another checkup again."

Aaliyah blushed. "Of course, I'll let you. I want you to be there with me."

"What did the doctor say...is everything good with our baby?"

"So far so good. My blood pressure was a little on the high side, so the doctor told me to take it easy. Other than that, our baby is perfect."

"The high blood pressure is all on me. I promise not to bring any more stress to your life. I'll be a perfect gentleman. Whatever you need, tell me and I'll make sure to deliver."

"Everything I need is standing right in front of me," Aaliyah said moving closer to Dale.

"I don't deserve your forgiveness but I'll be eternally grateful for it." Dale placed his hand under Aaliyah's chin and lifted it up so their eyes were locked. "From the bottom of my heart, I'm so sorry for what I put you through and the pain I caused your family. I will spend the rest of my life making it up to you."

Dale leaned down and pressed his lips against Aaliyah's. She took in the faint scent of his cologne, she'd been longing for. When Dale eased away, Aaliyah pulled him back in, kissing him harder and with more vigor.

"You're back home where you belong," Aaliyah said between intense kisses while unbuttoning Dale's shirt. They undressed each other with patience but each touch of their lips was filled with undying passion. Once Aaliyah was clad in only her vintage rose Chantilly lace & mesh plunge bra with matching cheekster panty, Dale scooped her up and in his arms. He carried her to the bedroom, laying her down on the bed.

Aaliyah had lust and love in her eyes as Dale stood over her. Neither wanted to engage in foreplay. They craved for the same thing. Dale wanted to get lost in her wetness and Aaliyah wanted to feel every inch of him inside of her. He unclipped her bra as she slid out her panties. Both let out a deep moan as their bodies became one.

"I love you, Aaliyah." Dale spoke with a certainty that resonated with her. Any doubts Aaliyah had, were now put to rest.

"I love you too. Now and forever." Dale leaned down and once again he and Aaliyah exchanged fiery kisses, making love as if this may be their last time in each other's arms.

"I was fuckin' shocked when my mother said you called. I ain't heard from you or seen you since your dad's funeral," Shayla said as her and Taren shared a blunt.

"Yeah, I went into a little depression after my dad got murdered," Taren sighed becoming somber thinking about her father and smoking weed only made it worse.

"I feel you. Ya was real close and shit. After all these years they still ain't arrest nobody for his murder," she said shaking her head. "My mother go to his gravesite at least three times a month. His death hit her hard too, especially since that was her only brother," Shayla continued doing a puff-puff-pass.

"True, Aunt Bernice is probably the only other person who understand my pain."

"He was my blood too," Shayla barked.

"Calm down, cuz. I know you loved my dad

but when he got killed you wasn't even living at home. You had been gone for a few years. My mother fell completely apart so Aunt Bernice was the only person I could share my grief with, 'cause she was grieving too."

"That make sense. I'm sorry about yo' mom too. Losing mom and dad, that shit gotta be hard."

"It is but I'm finding ways to deal wit' it. That's one of the reasons I came back to Miami," Taren revealed. "It's crazy because I remembered hearing you had moved out this way but wasn't sure if you were still here. When Aunt Bernice said you were and then when I spoke to you and you told me you were working at a strip club, I felt like that was a sign."

"So, what you mean by finding ways to deal and it's why you back in Miami?" Shayla questioned starting to become faded.

"One of the people responsible for my father's murder lives in Miami."

"Word! You neva told me you knew who killed my uncle. Does my mother know?"

"Nope. I didn't wanna say shit until I had it handled. Remember when I said I needed a favor," Taren reminded her cousin.

"Yep. You wanted to stay here at my apartment and get you a job at the strip club I work at. But umm, you didn't need no help wit' that. When the boss saw them titties you were working wit', he hired that ass on the spot," Shayla laughed.

"Ain't these joints nice," Taren giggled, doing a quick jiggle with her breasts. "But on a serious tip, this next favor is the most important one of them all."

"Shoot. I got yo' back. We family," Shayla stated before giving Taren a blow-back. After exhaling the smoke into her cousin's mouth, Shayla was so lit she would've agreed to anything.

"Cool. I'm glad you all in. You exactly what I need to pull this shit off," Taren smiled.

It was no accident Taren sought out her cousin to assist with her plan. Shayla was a few years older than Taren but not nearly as seasoned, although she didn't know it. Shayla had been running the streets, tricking niggas out of cash and dabbling in other side hustles for years. She was under the impression Taren was the naïve one out of the two of them. She had no idea, her scamming was on some low level, petty shit compared to her cousin's wicked ways. She would soon learn because Taren was about to bring Shayla to the dark side.

Chapter Eleven

Never Letting Go

"Babe, do you know this is the first time you came and sat through one of my training sessions," Darien said, grabbing the towel and wiping the sweat off his forehead.

"Thanks for sharing your observation," Angel said sarcastically. "Are you trying to imply I'm a bad wife by making that comment?"

"Sounds like you have a guilty conscious,"

Darien cracked, giving Angel a kiss. "And it wouldn't matter if you never came to a practice. It wouldn't stop me from thinking I have the most amazing wife ever."

"Darien Blaze for the win. Good save," Angel winked.

"No save needed. Only speaking the truth about my beautiful, intelligent wife," Darien enthused placing his arm around Angel's waist.

"I'm pretty lucky myself. When you were doing those shoulder presses and walking lunges, my gosh every muscle in your body was on full flex. To think, I go to sleep and wake up with those muscles wrapped around my body," Angel teased.

"I guess that means we're mutually enamored with each other. Some say that's rare, so we're both lucky."

"Yes, we are," Angel agreed, admiring how sexy her championship hubby looked even while drenched in sweat. "I'm sure you've worked up an appetite. Do you want to go get something to eat?"

"You already know. Let's go upstairs, so I can take a shower and then go eat at a restaurant of your choice and do some shopping afterwards.

I haven't bought you any new jewelry recently. I need to change that today."

Angel raised an eyebrow at Darien. "You're in a very generous mood today, what gives?"

"For one, I missed you and I want to show you how much."

"You showed me last night when my flight got in. We were practically undressed by the time we got to the hotel."

"That was the best mistake I've ever made in my life. I'm not even supposed to be having sex when I'm training for a fight," Darien divulged. "But when you showed up looking like an early Christmas present, I couldn't resist." He gave a half smile remembering the sequin lace bodysuit and the destructed hourglass jeans Angel was wearing that accentuated her figure perfectly.

"I'm glad you couldn't resist," Angel blushed.

"Maybe if I keep showing you how much I love having you here with me, you'll decide to stay longer instead of going back to Miami."

"You might end up getting what you want."

"Really?! You staying? I'd be thrilled but I'm surprised. Just last week you were saying you wanted to spend some time with Aaliyah and focus on Angel's Girls."

"I still do, I mean I did. Aaliyah sent me a text last night. Her and Dale are back together so she no longer needs that shoulder to cry on, which is a good thing."

"What, how did that happen?"

"The text was brief. Aaliyah didn't go into details but said she had her mother to thank. My dad always says Precious can be a very persuasive woman when need be. Seems she came through for her daughter."

"Can't be mad at that. Glad it worked out. Dale seemed to be good people. I was shocked when you told me how things went down at the wedding. He didn't strike me as that type of dude but then again, he was runnin' off emotions, without knowing all the facts."

"Yeah, hopefully this is a new beginning for them. Speaking of new beginnings, it might be time for me to say peace out to Angel's Girls."

"Hold up," Darien stopped midway to the elevator. "I've been tryna get you to give up on that business for months. You finally decided to listen to your husband?"

"Not quite," Angel giggled. "I'm more so tired of listening to Desmond's mouth."

"Wait a minute. I like Desmond."

"I like him too. I just don't like his wife."

"When Desmond get married and to who? I come to Vegas to train for a fuckin' fight and all type of shit pop off."

"Justina. It was very recent. I still don't know what the rush was. I guess they're just so in love," Angel mocked, rolling her eyes.

"Aaliyah's best friend…this shit gets more and more interesting," Darien chuckled pushing the elevator door button up.

"I'm glad you find this humorous," Angel shook her head not amused. "Before I caught my flight last night, I met with Desmond. He came up with the great idea to have his new bride work at Angel's Girls and because of the contract we signed, he has every legal right."

"I'm all for you gettin' out that Madame of Miami life but leaving to be with me is one thing but handing over the business you started because you don't wanna work with your partner's wife is kinda weak. And you ain't no weak chick. You the most resilient woman I've ever met. One of the reasons I fell in love with you."

"Only you can clown me and compliment me in the same breath," Angel joked, playfully kissing Darien on his cheek.

"I'm not clowning you, babe. You always been your own boss and I ain't neva known you to let another person dictate your moves. No sense in starting that shit now."

"You're right," Angel agreed as the elevator doors opened and the couple stepped off. "I can't let my dislike for Justina make me abandon the company baring my name. That's just crazy," Angel huffed, looking at a text message that came through. "OMG...I was right," she mumbled.

"Right about what?" Darien questioned, entering their hotel suite.

"This girl named Nesa who contacted me about Justina, she's dead."

"Dead?!"

"Yes. Her friend Clarissa just hit me up. The woman found in the lake a few weeks ago was Nesa. My gut told me it was her but I didn't wanna believe it."

"That's unfortunate. I guess whatever secrets you thought Nesa might've had, died with her."

"Not if I have anything to do with it. It can't be a coincidence this woman who had dirt on Justina also worked for Desmond and now she's dead."

"Please don't start with the conspiracy the-ories," Darien blustered, turning on the knob in the shower. "Do you really hate Justina to the point you wanna stick a murder on her and Desmond?" he continued as he got undressed.

"I'm not sticking anything on anybody," Angel shot back. "I just wanna find out what happened to Nesa."

"That's called a police matter. It's their job to solve murders, not yours. Don't create problems where there aren't none. Leave it alone, Angel," Darien insisted before closing the shower door.

Angel brushed off Darien's warnings. She knew he meant well but that was of no consequence to her. Although there wasn't proof Justina and Desmond had anything to do with Nesa's murder, Angel wouldn't let it go, until she got confirmation, one way or the other.

"Baby, I'm so glad you're home!" Justina was clinging onto Desmond tightly.

"I'm happy to see you too." Desmond stroked Justina's hair then gave her a sweet kiss. "It's so cute how needy you seem. I guess now that we're married, you don't feel the need to play hard to get," he joked.

"I guess you haven't heard," Justina said nervously.

"Heard what?"

"They found Nesa's body. She was murdered but I'm sure you already knew that." Justina wanted a glass of wine, a shot, anything to calm her nerves but knew it was out of the question since she was with child. Instead she fidgeted with her hands and hair.

"Nesa is dead? What are talking about?" Desmond walked over to Justina who was now sitting on the couch with a frantic look of despair spread across her face.

"A few weeks ago, a woman's body washed up and they finally identified the woman as Nesa. What if the cops are able to trace her murder back to you?"

"That ain't gonna happen."

"How can you be sure? I'm positive you didn't think her dead body would wash up either but it did," Justina said pressing her hands against her head. "Desmond, I wouldn't be able to survive if you went to jail. I can't lose you," she cried, sounding panicked.

"Baby, calm down. You're not gonna lose me and I'm not going to jail because I didn't kill Nesa.

Trust me, if I had, I would've made sure her body was never found."

"But you said you were gonna handle it."

"And I did. I called Nesa and we met up. I told her to give me a price. She did and I gave it to her. All Nesa wanted was money. Once she got it, she was ready to leave Miami. I had no reason to kill her." Desmond was adamant.

"If you didn't kill Nesa then who?" Justina was more baffled than ever.

"I have no fuckin' clue. When we met up, her bags were packed and she was leaving immediately. It was part of our deal. I made it clear to her she was never to contact you and especially Angel or she would come up missing," Desmond stated. "I told her in the future, if she ever needed anything to contact me directly and I would make sure she was straight. Nesa understood not to cross me. She knew I could be her best friend or worst enemy."

"I should feel relieved right now knowing you aren't responsible for Nesa's death but I'm not. What if my connection to her gets out and the man I hired to kill her but yet I ended up killing him," Justina sighed.

Desmond came up behind Justina and placed

his hands on her shoulders, as she stood staring out the massive windows. He had this way of making her feel safe, like no other person had ever done in Justina's life.

"Stop worrying. It's not good for you or our baby."

Justina placed her hands on top of Desmond's. "I love when you say our baby. I feel like I finally have a real family."

"Because we are a family and that means I will always protect you and our child. By any means necessary."

Justina turned to face Desmond and stared up at him. "I don't deserve you but you're mine and I'm never letting you go."

"I thought I would never wake up again with you holding me like this," Aaliyah said as her and Dale laid in bed watching the sun rise.

"I hate I ever made you feel like that. I know you forgive me but I'll never forgive myself. If only we could go back to the night of our engagement party."

"Why that night?" Justina sat up in the bed and asked Dale.

"That's the night I found out Supreme killed my brother. Now I wish I never knew," Dale disclosed.

"You found out the night of our engagement party...how?"

"Some stripper told me."

"Wait, some random stripper at our engagement party came up and told you my father shot your brother?"

"I can't remember exactly how the conversation went as some things are clearer than others. Then it was loud in the club. When she mentioned Emory and Supreme killing him, I kinda blacked out. All I wanted to do was..." Dale's voice trailed off.

"Confront me and kill my dad." Aaliyah completed Dale's thought for him.

"That was before I knew the truth. I feel like shit for even thinking like that."

"Stop being so hard on yourself," Aaliyah stroked Dale's face. "I'm more interested in finding out who this stripper was and how she found out about my father."

"Aaliyah, let it go. It doesn't matter. I want

to put all that fuckery behind us. We've been given a second chance at love and we're having a baby. None of that other shit matters," Dale said, wrapping his arms around the woman he loved and feeling blessed to have her back in his life.

It would've been easy for Aaliyah to do as Dale asked and put the nightmare behind them. But she now blamed this mysterious stripper for potentially ruining her life, by turning the man she loved against her. Not only did Aaliyah want payback against the stripper but also the person who revealed what was supposed to have remained a family secret.

Chapter Twelve

Over My Dead Body

"Can I help you?" Elsa smiled at the woman who walked through the office doors. She looked stunning in a white ruffled wrap dress with deep cold shoulders finished with flared elbow sleeves and a gold grosgrain tie belt. The tall, slim woman paired the dress with ornate jewel set vamps and twisted stiletto heels that was the exact same color as the belt and other accessories adorning her wrist, ears and neck. The jet black pixie cut and red vampy lip made her photoshoot perfection.

"Yeah, my name Shayla and I saw ya ad online. Ya supposed to be hiring," she smacked, chewing on her gum.

Elsa raised an eyebrow wondering how one woman could look like the epitome of class but open her mouth and prove it to be a lie. "Yes, well we've currently fulfilled all of our open spots. But thank you for stopping by," Elsa said politely.

"But wait..." Shayla started to object but was interrupted.

"Aren't you runway ready!" Justina paused for a second and stared Shayla up and down after walking in the building, making her own presence known.

"Thank you, girl," Shayla beamed, appreciating the compliment coming from a woman who was not only beautiful but was clearly rich based on the rock weighing down her finger, the designer bag in her hand and her overall appearance screaming money.

"Good morning, Mrs. Blackwell." Elsa put on her most professional voice while greeting Justina but wished she'd turn around and walk back out the door.

"Hi, Elsa," Justina replied but maintaining eye contact with Shayla. "You must be here because you want to be one of Angel's Girls. What's your name?"

"Shayla, and chile, yes! I need a position. You know what's up," Shayla put her hand on her hip, feeling like her and Justina were forming a bond.

"Mrs. Blackwell, can I speak with you for a moment," Elsa said politely.

"In a minute, Elsa. I'm busy."

"It can't wait. I need to talk to you now...it's about our boss, Angel!" Elsa persisted.

Justina cut her eyes at Elsa before turning her attention back to Shayla. "Excuse me for one moment, I'll be right back."

"No worries, I'll be right here waiting fo' you!" Shayla shouted as Justina was walking off to a back office with Elsa.

"What was so important you couldn't wait until I finished speaking with a potential new hire?"

"Angel has a very strict policy about the women who can work here."

"Okay, and your point?"

"The woman out there isn't a fit."

"Are we looking at the same woman because the chick is gorgeous. That chocolate beauty is going to bring in prime dollars."

"I thought so too until she opened her mouth. She has absolutely no class, whatsoever. Angel would never want her representing this company."

"Listen, Elsa, you have to broaden your scope of thinking. There is a very profitable market for a woman like Shayla."

"The men who use our services, are extremely successful, rich, many of them are powerful and good looking. They can have their pick of women. They don't want to be bothered with a tacky woman like the one out there," Elsa frowned.

"Your definition of tacky can be described as a colorful personality by someone else. Desmond gave me the current client list for Angel's Girls. There are several rappers and professional athletes. A lot of them prefer the company of women like Shayla. Hell, they're married to them or have babies with them. So, let's not be so judgmental, Elsa."

"Wow, you're the last person I thought would be fighting me on this," Elsa twisted her mouth.

"Why is that?"

"No offense, but you're like a walking Beverly Hills rich girl billboard. I'm taking a wild guess you've been described as a snob on more than one occasion. Again, no offense."

"No offense taken. Everything you just said might be true and that's why you need to listen to my opinion and act on it. As long as she passes the criminal background check, std and drug tests, then hire her. We need some variation up in here," Justina expressed, waving her arm around. "Just like everyone doesn't like vanilla ice cream, everyone doesn't want to fuck a prima donna. We're running an escort service not recruiting for a high society debutante ball," she taunted. "Our clients want a woman who will get their dicks hard. Shayla qualifies, enough said. If you have a problem with it, call my husband," Justina asserted, sashaying out the room.

"I hate you're leaving but I understand. Plus, I'm sure dad misses you because I know I am," Aaliyah said sadly to her mom.

"I'll miss you too but I'm leaving you in good hands," Precious beamed.

"You really outdid yourself. Only a few days ago, any future with Dale seemed bleak at best, now we're discussing new wedding dates. That wouldn't be possible without you. You're the most amazing mother ever," Aaliyah praised.

"Flattery will get you everywhere and anything," Precious blushed. "I really am happy it all worked out. I never want to see my beautiful baby girl in such pain, ever again. It broke my heart. I had to fix it and make it right."

"Besides me, you're the only one who thinks you made it right. Dad isn't thrilled about it at all."

"Don't tell him I told you, but if it wasn't for your father, I couldn't have made it right. Supreme gave me the proof to show Dale," Precious revealed.

"He did?!" Aaliyah looked at her mother stunned.

"Yes. Trust me, it wasn't easy but he came around. If Supreme was willing to give me what I needed to make Dale see the truth, it means he's willing to accept the two of you being together," Precious reasoned.

"Maybe you're right, at least I hope so. I want Dale and I to have what you and dad share.

You all have been through so much but yet with the good and bad the two of you always end up together."

"Supreme and I have had our share of ups and downs. But even in the midst of our worst storms, I always knew we were destined to end up together."

"I believe it's my destiny to spend the rest of my life with Dale. Especially now we're about to bring a baby into the world together. My life is perfect again."

"I'm so happy for you." Precious reached over and hugged Aaliyah. "Seeing your eyes sparkle again, knowing you're happy is what every parent wants for their child. I remember when you were born and holding you in my arms. Now you're this beautiful woman, becoming a mother yourself and I'm so proud of you."

"Thank you so much for saying that. You're always in my corner no matter what," Aaliyah smiled.

"And that will never change," Precious said wiping a single tear, trickling down her cheek. "I would love to keep this mother & daughter conversation going but I need to leave so I can catch my flight."

"I love having you here with me but I know you have to go," Aaliyah said holding her mom's hand as she walked her to the door.

"Don't hesitate to call if you need me, I'll be on the first flight back. And make sure you follow your doctor's advice. Take it easy. I'm serious. I don't want anything happening to you or my grandchild. I love you, Aaliyah."

"I love you too." Aaliyah blew a kiss and waved goodbye, missing her mother already.

"Angel, thank goodness you finally called. It's been ridiculous over here," Elsa complained.

"I've been running around with Darien all day, so I just had time to return your call. What's the problem?"

"Justina," Elsa huffed. "It seems like she's hired every ratchet chick that's walked through the doors."

"Justina has...are you sure we're talking about the same person? She's one of the most arrogant women I've ever met."

"Exactly. She comes across as such an elitist but I swear as long as they have 'the look' as

Justina calls it, then she wants me to give them the greenlight."

"Justina doesn't have final approval on who we hire so don't stress it."

"But Desmond does and his wife is quick to remind me."

"Desmond is cosigning on her picks?"

"Yes. All except for one because she had an extensive criminal record. Felony assault, larceny, robbery, just to name a few. At this rate, Angel's Girls will be the go to place for every hoodrat in Miami," Elsa cracked.

"I'll be back next week but until then let me speak to Desmond," Angel said.

"Great, I'll just try and stay out of Justina's way until then."

"Okay, I'll talk to you later." Angel hung up with Elsa and immediately called Desmond.

"Hello."

"Desmond, it's me Angel. How are you?"

"Good and you? Are you enjoying your time in Vegas?" Desmond asked, leaning back in his office chair, staring out the window admiring the Miami skyline view.

"Vegas is great. I'm really enjoying spending time with Darien."

"Nice. Make sure you tell him I said hello and I expect some prime seats for his upcoming fight."

"Will do but I'm sure he already set some aside for you. But I didn't call to discuss Vegas. I wanted to see how everything has been going with Angel's Girls."

"Wonderful," Desmond answered confidently.

"Really. I know you wanted to move forward with interviewing potential new girls but I was under the impression you wouldn't actually do any hiring, until I got back from Vegas."

"Angel, when you sought me out to partner with you, one of the reasons, was so you had someone to run the business when you're unavailable. Let me do my job."

"It seems as if Justina is doing your job, not you," Angel scolded.

Desmond let out a slight chuckle. "Is that what Elsa told you. Listen, every woman Justina selected got my approval before they were hired."

"Did you hire them simply because your wife told you to? Did you even care if they were qualified?"

"Justina understands when it comes to business, I'm going to always do what's best for our company. Besides them being able to perform in the bed, what other qualifications do you want these women to have?"

"My girls represent me. They're supposed to be attractive, smart, articulate and the epitome of class. Being able to perform in bed, is simply an added bonus that gets them paid."

"No, it's the only reason they get paid. In the last two weeks, since Justina stepped in and hired these new women, our profits have tripled. We needed to bring some fresh new girls in the mix. My wife is doing an excellent job. She clearly has an eye for what our male clientele desires."

"Oh, there is no doubt in my mind, Justina knows how to play men. But I'm not a man, so I can't be played," Angel snapped.

"It's unfortunate you can't separate your personal feelings towards Justina for the greater good of the company. If you like, I'll be more than happy to buy you out. Name your price," he countered.

"There isn't one. I'll be back in the office tomorrow. See you then," Angel said, slamming the phone down.

"Baby, you okay?" Darien asked coming into

the bedroom right as Angel hung up the phone. "You seem upset."

"I have to get back to Miami."

"I thought you weren't leaving until next week. What happened…why do you have to leave all of sudden?"

"Justina is out of control and I have to put a stop to it before Desmond allows his wife to ruin my company," Angel seethed.

"Calm down. Whatever is going on at work, I'm sure can wait another week."

"Aren't you the one who told me I'm the boss. I make the rules. Well, I can't do that from Vegas."

"Baby, everyone knows Angel Girl's is your company."

"Then why did Desmond just offer to buy me out…huh?!"

"I'm sure you misunderstood him," Darien reasoned.

"I didn't misunderstand shit. That manipulative wife of his, is probably the one who gave Desmond the idea. If I stay gone much longer, the company will no longer be called Angel's Girls, it will be Justina's Girls. Over my dead body!"

Chapter Thirteen

Small World

"Man, that fuckin' Elsa chick get on my damn nerves," Shayla complained to Taren while getting dressed for work. "She lucky I'ma classy bitch or I would've smacked her by now."

"She still giving you a hard time?" Taren asked as she got ready to work the strip club.

"Yes. I swear if it won't for the girl Justina I told you about, I wouldn't have this job. Elsa wannabe cock blocking ass."

"Play nice wit' this Elsa broad. You don't wanna do nothing that might get you fired. Has Angel gotten back yet?"

"No, from what I understand she still out of town. Not sure when she coming back. I can't wait to lay eyes on the heifa who got my uncle killed."

"Shayla, don't fuck this up. Keep your cool. I'll let you know when it's time to make our move on Angel."

"Don't worry about me. I ain't gonna mess this up. I wanna make sure that chick get everything she deserve and then some."

"Cool and try to get in good with Justina. She might end up being useful."

"I can do that."

"I'm still wondering why Justina is working for Angel. She doesn't strike me as being the help type."

"I think I overheard Elsa saying something 'bout Justina being married to Angel's partner. So, nah, she ain't the help."

"You never mentioned that before," Taren stopped right in the middle of applying her lashes.

"I didn't think it was important. I told you she seemed rich," Shayla shrugged.

"Justina comes from money, so I ain't pay

you no mind when you made that comment. But Angel's partner is Desmond which means Justina is his wife. What a fuckin' small world. This might make things a little more complicated but I'll make it work," Taren said thinking about Dominique who was also on her hit list.

When Justina entered the strip club, it was her intent to head directly to her husband's office. But when she noticed, what she referred to as Desmond's charity case, all that changed. It was one thing for Justina to battle her nemesis in the daylight. It was different seeing Dominique on her turf, which was the stage because she owned it and that had Justina feeling some type of way. In her clothes, she looked like a petite little thing but being damn near naked, you could see Dominique was plump in all the right places. Not only that, she knew how to move her body. Unlike most of the other strippers, Dominique was truly a talented dancer and it showed.

"Damn, it felt so good to be back on stage!" Dominique shouted after her set was over and she walked off.

"It's good to have you back and of course you killed it up there," one of the other dancers cheered. "Before I forget, Desmond said come to his office once you finished your set."

"Thanks, I'll go see him now." Dominique was feeling like a star. Smiling and waving at people while passing them on her way to Desmond's office. "Hey! I heard you wanted to see me," she smiled walking in wearing basically her birthday suit.

"Don't you know how to knock," Justina popped when Dominique came in. "And do you always parade around naked in front of married men?"

"Most of the men who come to this strip club are married, so I guess that would be yes," Dominique popped back.

"Well this married man isn't one of your customers, so put some fuckin' clothes on." Justina stepped forward with fire in her eyes and Desmond already knew what that meant.

"Here, put this on," he said handing Dominique a jacket one of his security guys left in his office.

"Thank you."

"Dominique, wait for me in the hallway,

while I finish up talking to my wife."

"Sure." Dominique could feel Justina burning a hole in her back as she walked out.

"That disrespectful bitch," Justina fumed.

"Baby, this is a strip club and Dominique just got off stage."

"Are you defending her?"

"All I'm saying is, she's used to being naked, so it probably didn't even cross her mind to cover up before coming in my office," Desmond explained.

"So, these strippers just prance around you all day naked? It's one thing for them to be on the stage but can't they at least be professional and cover the fuck up when they come into the boss's office?" Justina was steaming.

"Do you have a problem with all the dancers being around me naked, or is it just Dominique?"

"It's no secret how I feel about Dominique but I find it disrespectful for any of them to be coming in here naked, unless that's what you want," Justina said in an accusatory tone.

"Honestly, I never thought about it. I own a strip club. At this point in my life, seeing naked women doesn't move me one way or the other. But I'm a married man now and you're my wife.

I never want you to feel disrespected. For now on, besides you, no naked women in my office... okay." Desmond had one arm around Justina's waist and the other was lifting up her chin so she would look at him.

"Okay but I doubt you'll want to see me naked much longer. I can tell I'm putting on weight. My clothes aren't fitting me like they used to," Justina complained.

"Baby, you're pregnant. You're supposed to gain weight and I always love seeing you naked. You're the only woman I desire."

"You mean that?" Justina needed reassurance.

"Yes. Justina, I'm in love with you. You're my wife. I want you and only you. Don't ever doubt that."

"I didn't realize being pregnant was going to have me feeling so insecure. It's taking me back to when I was an awkward teenager and Aaliyah stole..." Justina put her head down, not wanting to remember that time in her life.

"Aaliyah stole your boyfriend? Hmmm, isn't that what you were gonna say? Justina, you are no longer that awkward teenager, although I doubt you ever were. You're a beautiful, sexy woman.

But most importantly, I'm not Amir. Nobody can take me away from you. I'm yours. See that ring on your finger and this one on mine," Desmond held up his hand. "It means we belong to each other and no one else."

"You're right. These pregnancy hormones have me going crazy."

"No, you just crazy in love and so am I," Desmond said putting his lips on Justina's. It was supposed to be a quick, sweet kiss but the wetness of her mouth made him kiss a little more and a little longer. Soon those kisses turned into Desmond laying Justina down on his desk and slowly lifting up her skirt. He slipped off her panties so he could taste how sweet the lips between her legs were.

"Oh, baby...ah, that feels so good," Justina moaned breathlessly. Although his dick was rock hard and he wanted to be drenched inside her juices, knowing how much pleasure his tongue was giving his wife made Desmond wait a little longer. But once Justina's body started shaking from the orgasm she received, Desmond made her cum again when he slid deep inside, filling up her walls until the pleasure and pain had her screaming out his name.

"It must be nice being back home and not living out of a hotel but then again your suite was bigger than most people's apartment," Angel commented to Aaliyah while sitting outside by the pool having lunch.

"I did miss this place but it didn't feel like home when Dale wasn't here. That's why I stayed at the hotel. Now that we're a family again, there's no other place I would rather be," Aaliyah smiled.

"I really am happy it all worked out for you, Aaliyah. You're glowing. Happiness and pregnancy suites, you well."

"I think so too. I can't wait until I really start showing. Like if I lift up my shirt you can see a slight bulge but I'm ready for my belly to poke out and I have to wear maternity clothes. I saw the cutest little Tiffany Rose dress for pregnant women. I can't wait to wear it!" Aaliyah gushed. "When are you and Darien going to have a little one running around?"

"No time soon. We have plenty of time to start a family."

"If you hurry, your little girl or boy can grow

up with me and Justina's kids."

"Justina is pregnant too?"

"Yep! Isn't that awesome. Me and my best friend are pregnant at the same time. I'm a little further along than her but our kids will definitely be besties too."

"Desmond told me they got married but nothing about the pregnancy," Angel said wondering to herself why he didn't mention it.

"When Justina told me, she had only recently found out. You were in Vegas for a long time. Now that you're back, I'm sure Desmond will tell you or maybe even Justina. She told me she's working at Angel's Girls now. How do you feel about that? I know she's not one of your favorite people."

"Justina is okay, she just rubs me the wrong way sometimes." Angel did her best to play down her detest for Aaliyah's bestie.

"Justina has her ways but she's a sweetheart once you get to know her. Me, her and Amir all kinda come from the same world. Very entitled and it can be a turn off sometimes but we're harmless," Aaliyah laughed.

"I'm sure you're right." Angel didn't want to make Aaliyah aware just how much she mistrusted Justina. Mainly because she didn't want her to be forewarned. Aaliyah wouldn't do it purposely but Angel needed Justina to put her guard down in order to catch her fucking up. "I meant to ask you, did you ever figure out how Dale found out about his brother?" she questioned.

"OMG...yes! Some stripper told him at our engagement party."

"Did he tell you the stripper's name?"

"No. He said it was some random broad. Dale wants me to let it go but I'm determined to find out who this chick is and how she found out."

"I don't blame you," Angel agreed. She was more positive than ever Nesa was the messenger and Justina was the one who supplied her with the dirt.

"Whoever is responsible is going to pay. My wedding and my relationship with Dale was almost destroyed behind that bullshit." Aaliyah's rage was brewing.

"Take it easy, Aaliyah. I can see how upset you're getting. I should've never brought it up."

"I'm glad you did. I needed someone to vent to. Dale wants to forget it ever happened and Justina agrees with him. Whenever I bring it up she changes the subject," Aaliyah griped.

I'm sure she does. It's because Justina's the one

responsible for wrecking your wedding and almost ruining your relationship with Dale but how do I prove it, Angel thought to herself. *I can't bring my suspicions to Aaliyah without proof. She'll think I'm being bias since it's no secret I'm not a fan of Justina. Nesa was the key but now that she's dead I have to figure out another way to connect her to Justina and possibly Nesa's murder.*

Chapter Fourteen

Make Things Right

"I have the perfect girl for you. I'm heading into the office now. Give me a few minutes and I'll send you her picture when I get to my desk," Justina told one of Angel's Girls newest clients as she was getting out her car.

"Mrs. Blackwell, hey!" Shayla waved coming out the office building.

"Hello, Shayla, how are you this morning?"

Justina asked being cordial but not friendly.

"I'm doing alright. I came to speak to Elsa 'cause the last week she ain't been gettin' me no clients and I wanted to see what was up. First things were poppin' and now it's dead," Shayla complained. "A girl got bills to pay."

"You know what, I just got off the phone with a new client. I was going to give it to another girl but I think you'll be perfect."

"Foreal! You do that for me?!"

"Why not. All your feedback from clients has been great so far and you'll be a good fit for this guy. Don't make me regret my decision, so be on your best behavior."

"I promise, I will. Thanks for lookin' out. I know I wouldn't neva even been hired if it won't for you. You nothin' like Elsa say you is," Shayla casually mentioned.

"What exactly did Elsa say?"

"I just overheard her complaining to Angel about how you runnin' the business."

"Angel's back?" Justina was surprised to learn.

"Yes, she introduced herself when she came in. She said she was the owner. But um, please don't mention to Elsa what I said. She dying for an excuse to fire me."

"Don't worry about it, Shayla. I won't say a word. I'll call you later on and give you the details regarding the client you'll be meeting tonight."

"Thanks, girl. Talk to you later!" Shayla grinned putting her sunglasses on, feeling she had scored some points with Justina.

Justina hurried inside, glad Shayla gave her the heads up Angel was back. Justina believed she had at least another week of running things the way she wanted but with Angel's return that would all change.

"Good morning! How are you today?" Justina made sure to sound extra cheerful.

"I'm doing fine. You seem to be in a jovial mood this morning." Elsa was surprised since normally Justina barely acknowledged her existence.

"I'm actually in a great mood. I was thinking I could order us some breakfast...my treat. What do you say?"

"I would say that isn't necessary," Angel came from around the corner and said. "It'll be my treat."

"Angel, I had no idea you were back. I thought you were staying in Vegas for at least another week or two." Justina did a wonderful job pretending she didn't know Angel was in the building.

"Yeah, I had to cut my trip short."

"I'm sure your husband was disappointed."

"He was but luckily Darien is very understanding. He knows I have a business to run."

"Wonderful! Speaking of business, let me go in my office and get some work done. Elsa, I still owe you breakfast. Let me know when," Justina smiled, appearing to be a model employee.

"Justina, before you go, can I speak with you in my office?" Aaliyah asked.

"Sure. Let me put my stuff down and I'll be right back."

"Who is the woman that showed up today?" Elsa remarked to Angel when Justina walked off. "Dare I say she was pleasant."

"If Justina's pleasant, it only means she's up to something. I'll be in my office waiting for her arrival," Angel sniped.

Justina took her time getting situated after being summoned to Angel's office. She checked emails, made a couple of calls and sent a few pics of Shayla to the new client before finally making her way to Angel.

"I apologize for taking so long but I had to

handle a few things," Justina explained.

"No problem. Close the door please." Angel's voice was anything but pleasant, still Justina obliged her request. "You can have a seat," she continued after the door was closed.

"Is there a problem, Angel? Your voice is a bit intense."

"I just don't like when outsiders come into my company and try to make decisions that isn't best for business."

"I want Angel's Girls to be a huge success too. Desmond is part owner and since I'm his wife, I suppose that makes me an owner too. My intentions are always what is best for business."

"Justina, you're married to Desmond not me. I don't give a damn what arrangement the two of you have. The final say so for what goes down at the company I started, is me. The women you hired while I was gone, don't represent my brand."

"Numbers don't lie. The women I brought in, are bringing in triple compared to your other girls. I get you don't like me, Angel. I don't like you either. But don't allow your pride to get in the way of making a profit."

"Since we have a mutual dislike for each other, why are you working here? You don't need the money. Is it to simply irritate the fuck outta me?"

"My husband wanted me to manage his share of the business in his absence. Desmond is running one successful strip club here and about to open another one. It's my duty as his wife to try and ease the stress. So, when he asked me to step in, I agreed," Justina stated.

"I have the perfect solution to ease everyone's stress...Quit! Let me run my business and you all can just cash checks. Win, win for everyone."

"I'm not going anywhere, Angel. If you can't work with me, then you quit. Desmond will be more than happy to make you a very generous offer. I'll leave you to marinate on that because I have deals to close."

Angel wanted to jump over the desk and put her fist down Justina's throat but knowing she was with child made her press pause. Instead she let her walk out the door and Angel began devising a plan to get rid of her adversary once and for all.

"Desmond, thank you for seeing me man. I've been wanting to sit down with you for a minute but I figured I was the last person you wanted to see," Dale said, unable to shake his guilt. "I hate myself for what I did to you."

Desmond and Dale met for dinner at Casa Tua South Beach. They were seated on the second floor that was allotted for members. The upscale Italian restaurant was the perfect spot for them to meet as it had delicious food, wine but most importantly gave them the privacy they both wanted.

"I was wondering what took you so long to invite me out for dinner," Desmond stated coolly. "Listen, we go way back no need to hate yourself for making a mistake."

"A mistake that could've cost you your life."

"True and that's what I'm thankful for. I'm alive and not dead. I'm also thankful the bullet missed your intended target. Aaliyah can forgive a lot of things but I don't think killing her father, in front of her face, is one of them."

"Who you telling," Dale shook his head. "I completely fucked up."

"You did. So, save all your apologizing for your woman. No need to ask for my forgiveness, it's already yours. No need to speak on it," Desmond wanted to make clear.

"I don't deserve it but I appreciate you saying that, man. I'm lucky to have you as a friend. I can trust you. I can't say that about many people, including Aaliyah."

"I was under the impression you and Aaliyah worked everything out. I was gonna wait for you to tell me but Justina even said you all were expecting a baby."

"It's true we are but..." Dale stopped himself from continuing his thought but Desmond knew him well enough to have an idea what had Dale in a bad place.

"You're upset Aaliyah didn't come to you when she found out Supreme was the one who killed Emory."

"Before you say anything, I understand it's her father and she wanted to protect him. But I'm her husband or at least we were supposed to be married by now. Shouldn't her loyalty be to me?"

"Did you ever think that maybe Aaliyah wasn't trying to protect her father, she was trying to protect you."

"Protect me? How was she protecting me?" Dale wanted to know.

"Look how long it took for you to accept the truth about Emory's connection to Maya and Arnez. Aaliyah probably knew you would've overreacted and not believed her. Then you would've sought retribution against her father. But you and I both know going up against Supreme would've meant you were a dead man. Even if you got to him first, somebody within Supreme's circle would have made sure you ended up six feet under too. Do you think Aaliyah wanted to bury the man she loved and have your blood on her hands?"

"I never considered anything you just said but your points are all valid." Dale put down his utensils and pushed his plate away. He lost his appetite. "I was consumed with believing Aaliyah didn't really love me and her loyalty was to her family, not me. But she does love me," he said as if realizing this for the first time. 'Thank you for opening up my fuckin' eyes. I'm 'bout to ruin my second chance with the woman I love, before we even have a chance to make it."

"That's the beautiful thing about life. As long as you are alive you still have time to make it right. Go make things right with Aaliyah."

"Angel's ass is finally back!" Taren said salivating at the mouth. "I'm tempted to do a drive by and riddle her body with bullets and leave her on the side of the road like they did my daddy."

"Cuz, I'm new to all this murder shit but I don't think that's the right move. The police will have you in handcuffs before you can even reach Interstate 95," Shayla smacked. "I think we need to plan this out a lil' betta."

Taren was operating on emotions and knew she needed to listen to her cousin. "You right."

"Glad you think so. I mean what's the point of killin' her if you gon' end up behind bars in the process. We can figure out how to get rid of that ass and get away wit' it. Ya feel me?"

"I do," Taren nodded. "Plus, I wanna have some fun wit' Angel before I put her down to rest. You've given me a great idea on how I can get rid of two problems at once," Taren said with a wicked smile on her face.

Chapter Fifteen

She's Back

When the private jet arrived at the exclusive landing strip outside of LaLuna, St. George's, Grenada, Aaliyah was mesmerized. Their final destination was Spice Island, one of the Caribbean's lushest isles and a little known gem. It was an intimate Italian owned resort on a private estate in the Morne Rouge area. Set around a scenic cove with outdoor suites, hillside cottages and a beachfront villa where Dale and Aaliyah would be calling home for the next few weeks.

"I've never seen such a beautiful island. It's breathtaking," Aaliyah gasped. "It feels magical."

"I thought you would love it but I'm glad I was right. It was important to me, I brought you someplace where you felt special."

"Dale, I always feel special when I'm with you." Aaliyah cupped Dale's face in the palm of her hand.

"I haven't been fair to you, Aaliyah. I apologized and begged for your forgiveness but deep down, I had felt this sort of resentment, thinking your heart wasn't all the way in it. That you would rather protect your family then trust in our love."

'That isn't true, Dale," Aaliyah was quick to deny.

"I know that now. It's crazy because it took me having a conversation with Desmond and seeking his forgiveness, for me to realize I had it all wrong. He made me see the truth and now I can truly say, I'm ready to make you my wife, be a husband to you and a father to our child. Aaliyah, will you marry me? My heart is one hundred percent in."

Dale was once again on bended knee holding a wedding ring but unlike the first time there were no dark secrets lingering in the background. There wasn't any hesitation or self doubt. They had survived the storm and instead of tearing them apart, it made their love even stronger but most importantly, they were committed for better for worse.

"Yes! Yes! I'll marry you. You're the only man I want to spend my life with...forever!"

Dale slid the diamond ring on Aaliyah's finger. "I wanted you to have a new ring to signify our new beginning."

"It's even more beautiful than the other ring," she teared up and said. "This time nothing will stop us from getting married."

"To make sure of that, we'll be getting married tonight...here," Dale said.

Aaliyah's eyes brightened up as if they were filled with stars. "We're getting married tonight?! Are you serious?" she asked eagerly.

"Yes. I made all the arrangements, with the hope you'd say yes to my proposal," Dale grinned, showcasing the most perfect set of teeth, which always made Aaliyah want to put her tongue in his mouth.

"When you smile at me like that, I can never resist you. Come over here and give me a kiss." That was the first kiss of many more throughout the rest of the evening.

The lovebirds exchanged I do's on a quiet corner of the beach, amid romantic touches like a chiffon draped arch, candlelit floor lanterns, oversized throw pillows matching the wedding color scheme of sandy neutrals, custom gold with teal blues. After the ceremony, they had dinner on the Ocean Room Terrace, then dancing the night away under the stars as husband and wife.

"There's my beautiful wife!"

"Omigosh, baby! What are you doing here and you brought flowers," Justina beamed kissing Desmond. "Let me close the door. We have some nosey people in here. They don't need to see me undressing my husband at the workplace," she giggled flirtatiously.

"I would love to be inside of you right now," Desmond whispered in Justina's ear while sliding his hand up her inner thigh and moving her silk panties to the side.

"Ah," Justina moaned in pleasure when he made her wet with a teasing finger fuck before stopping abruptly.

"I'll finish tonight when we get home," Desmond continued, licking her earlobe with his warm tongue.

"I hate you!" Justina pounced on her husband's chest. "How can you get me all excited like that then stop," she pouted.

"Baby, I'm really short on time. I had to leave out early this morning and you were sleeping, so I wanted to stop by and see your gorgeous face. I actually have a meeting I need to get to but if I didn't see you first, I wouldn't be able to focus."

"You always say the right things, plus these orchids and roses are everything."

"Yes, they are...just like you," Desmond said kissing Justina again.

"Don't start something you can't finish."

"You're right." Desmond stopped. "It's damn near impossible for me, to keep my hands off my sexy, beautiful wife but I'll try. You have your office decorated nice," he commented, switching the subject so both of them could get their minds off sex.

"Thank you. I tried to put a little glam touch

on it. Aaliyah even got me an office warming gift," Justina bragged. "Isn't it cute? She even had it framed for me," Justina said, pointing to a Boss Babe quote hanging on her wall.

When Life Gave Me Lemons, I Bought Some Sugar, Hired A Sales Team And Made Money. Duh.

"That sounds like something you and Aaliyah would appreciate," Desmond cracked.

"Yeah, we know each other probably better than anyone else. Well, almost," Justina thought about it and said. "You are the only person who really knows everything about me."

"As it should be. I'm your husband and best friend. But you seem to be in a good place with Aaliyah, which means you're healing and letting go of the hatred. I'm proud of you."

"Yeah, we had a heart to heart at the hospital after you and Supreme were shot. Both of our emotions were running high and I had just told Amir the truth about us. But during that conversation we had a break through. I no longer hate or want revenge against her and Amir for what they did to me. I guess that happens when you truly fall in love. So, thank you, my love."

"No, thank you. I used to think falling in love

was fluff for movies, television and books. Then I met this incredible woman who was unbelievably beautiful but complex as fuck. She stole my heart and never gave it back but I don't want it back."

"You ain't getting it back neither. It belongs to me and I'm so grateful. To think you could've died at that wedding because of something I caused, makes me cringe."

"What are you talking about? It wasn't your fault Dale shot me."

"I basically put the gun in his hand when I had Nesa tell him the truth about who shot his brother. My actions set in motion a disaster," Justina said with regret.

"Baby, let it go. I'm here with you. Dale and Aaliyah jetted off to a private island, got married and are enjoying an extended honeymoon. So, everything turned out the way it's supposed to be."

"You're right. We both married the men we love and we're pregnant at the same time," Justina gushed gleefully. "Our children will grow up together being best friends just like me and Aaliyah. It can't get any more perfect than that."

"Girl, I was surprised when you called. You haven't been here to get your hair done in so long," Kecia said to Clarissa when she sat down in her chair.

"You know I used to come with Aspen and after she got killed, I tried to stay away from everything that reminded me of her."

"Yeah, I was stunned when I heard about her death. She was good people. One of my favorite clients. Did the police finally arrest somebody, 'cause I never heard anything," Kecia wanted to know.

"Nope and I doubt there ever will be an arrest. I think Aspen's killer gon' end up getting street justice."

"Sometimes that's the best kind. You feel me?"

"For sure," Clarissa nodded.

"So, what we doing with this hair today? I see your haircut done grown all the way out," Kecia said combing through what used to be a tapered bob. "You got a lot of length now."

"I know right. At first, I was gonna have you cut it again because I loved that style but now I think I'ma try to let my hair grow out. So, you can braid it up and do a wig install," Clarissa said.

"You know what," Kecia said, turning the chair Clarissa was sitting in to face her. "You should let me do an old school sew in weave."

"A sew in? Girl, I ain't had a sew in, in forever. You still do those."

"Not really because everybody usually wants the lace front, closure installation. But a few weeks ago, a client came in and she wanted that Aaliyah swooped style, so I suggested we do a sew in to make it look more natural. Man, that shit came out so cold. I was impressed wit' myself," Kecia bragged.

"It looked good like that?!"

"Yes! I had that hair blending like it was growing from..." Kecia hesitated for a second trying to remember the name. "Nikki! That was her name. It look like it was growing from Nikki's scalp. I even took pictures, so you can see for yourself what I'm talking about."

"Chile, let me see. I'm about to walk outta here with a sew in, the way you talking."

"You damn sure are," Kecia popped proudly, going through the pics in her phone. "Here it is! Ain't this shit fire!"

Clarissa almost fell out the chair when she saw the face staring back at her. "That's Taren's trifling ass! She the evil bitch that killed Aspen and tried to kill my friend Dominique," she yelled.

Everyone in the salon turned to see who was the woman screaming at the top of her lungs. "Calm down, Clarissa." Kecia patted her on the shoulders. "I think there's some mistake. Her name is Nikki not Taren."

"Fuck that is! That ain't no Nikki. She must've lied and gave you a fake ass name. When was she in here? I want all the details. Shit! If Taren's in Miami that means Dominique in danger. Tell me what you know then I gots to go!" Clarissa barked, anxious to leave the salon and warn Dominique that Taren was back.

Chapter Sixteen

Basic Instinct

"Damn, why you ain't answering yo' fuckin' phone!" Clarissa yelled out loud while driving to Dominique's condo. Knowing Taren had been lurking around Miami all this time had her feeling on edge. She knew Taren had to be up to no good, which meant she had been laying low plotting. Clarissa was praying Dominique wasn't part of the plan.

After leaving multiple messages, Clarissa was relieved when she finally reached her destination. She rushed to Dominique's floor and immediately started banging on the door. "Oh shit," she mumbled when it flew open. *This ain't good*, Clarissa thought to herself, pulling out the only weapon she had in her purse, which was a Boker Kalashnikov Limited Edition Dagger Automatic Knife. She was ready to slit a throat if need be. Clarissa took off her heels so she couldn't be heard walking on the hardwood floors. As she tiptoed down the hall, her heart dropped when she saw traces of blood leading into Dominique's bedroom.

This can't be happening...this can't be happening, Clarissa kept saying to her herself, with tears swelling up in her eyes. Dominique's door was cracked slightly open. First, she stood with her back against the wall for a few seconds to see if she could hear any commotion. When there was nothing but silence, Clarissa prepared herself for the worse. She pushed open the door expecting to see Dominique's dead body but instead it was Mrs. Armstrong. She was lying on her stomach with three bullets in her back. From the smeared blood, it appeared her body had been dragged from the doorway entrance to the middle of the bedroom floor. Once Clarissa was positive the woman was deceased, she raced out the condo and didn't stop until she was back in her car with the doors locked. In the middle of her huffing and puffing she noticed Dominique calling.

"Hello!" Clarissa answered sounding out of breath.

"You alright...why you breathing so hard?" Dominique asked.

"'Cause I was running. Shit, I ain't ran that fast since I was on the track team in middle school."

"Running? I ain't never seen you run," Dominique laughed.

"Girl, ain't nothing funny, what I'm about to tell you." Clarissa finally got her breathing intact and her voice had turned super serious.

"Now you're scaring me." Dominique was no longer laughing. Instead she was gripping her phone, hanging onto every word Clarissa spoke.

"Where are you?"

"At the club. One of the dancers called me, asking if I could cover their afternoon shift because an emergency came up at the last minute. Why?"

"That phone call probably saved your life," Clarissa sighed and then continued with the bad news. "Mrs. Armstrong is dead and I believe Taren killed her." There was an eerie silence on the other end of the phone. "Hello! Hello!" Clarissa shouted. But Dominique had literally fell to the floor and passed out, after learning the fate of a woman who became almost like a mother figure to her, in so many ways.

"You sure she's dead?" Shayla questioned Taren, as she was driving them back to her apartment.

"Positive," Taren snapped, snatching off her wig, hat and sunglasses then tossing them in the backseat. "I can't believe this shit! I've been monitoring Dominique's schedule for weeks. This was supposed to be her day off."

"Why you have to kill that lady?" Shayla questioned, starting to think her cousin might be a little on the crazy side. She was onboard for killing Angel because Taren had her believing she was responsible for killing her uncle. But killing an old lady was never part of the plan, at least not the one Shayla agreed to participate in. Taren asked her to be the getaway driver, not an accessory to murder after the fact.

"I asked her to call Dominique and tell her she had to come back home asap but the dumb old hag refused," Taren scoffed. "She left me no choice but to kill her stupid ass."

Shayla side eyed Taren. She didn't see an ounce of remorse on her cousin's face. Her words were cold and steady. It sent a chill down Shayla's spine.

"So, what you gon' do about this Dominique chick? When she finds out the old lady dead, she ain't going back to that crib. She gon' move the fuck out."

"Just like I found this place, I'll find the new one. Dominique can't hide from me forever. This is gonna take a bit longer than I thought but I've mastered the skill of patience," Taren said staring straight ahead, escaping to the devilish dark world in her head.

"Babe, where are you rushing off to?" Justina questioned when she stepped out the shower and saw Desmond grabbing his car key.

"I have to go. Mrs. Armstrong was murdered."

"Who is Mrs. Armstrong?"

"The woman I hired to take care of Dominique."

"I didn't realize Dominique required personal assistance for her care."

"When she first got out the hospital, she did need a caretaker. After Dominique was physically better, I still wanted someone I trusted to stay and watch over her."

"I see. So, who murdered this woman...was it some sort of robbery?"

"Dominique was hysterical on the phone but from what she said, it was Taren."

"Taren, the woman who blew up your club?" Justina asked.

"Yes. Evidently, she sneaked back into Miami and went to the condo looking for Dominique. I'll have to find someplace else for her to stay. I just stopped Dominique's security detail a week ago because I thought she was safe, now I'll have to put them back on."

"Why do you feel so fuckin' responsible for this girl? She can find her own place to stay and get some of her homeboys to watch over her, if she needs protection so bad," Justina spit.

"I could but I'm not. I'm the one who brought Dominique to Miami to work at Diamond's &

Pearl. It's not her fault, she was in the wrong place at the wrong time and got caught up with someone as sadistic as Taren. She needs my protection and I'm gonna give it to her," Desmond stated.

"Fine, you go play superhero to your damsel in distress. But when I go find my own protector, don't expect me to explain shit."

"What the fuck did you just say to me?" Desmond grabbed Justina's wrist as she was turning to go back in the master bathroom.

"You heard what I said." Justina's glare was vicious. "If you think I'm going to sit around and let you play champion to another bitch, you don't know me at all."

Justina had been such the loving wife lately, Desmond had almost forgotten how treacherous she could be. But she made sure to remind him.

"Are you threatening to leave me or fuck around wit' another nigga?" Desmond asked Justina the question, like he wanted to have all the facts before he went in on that ass.

"Don't get it confused. Don't think because I'm in my second trimester, I can't pack my shit up and leave, or go get me another man, if that's what I choose to do. I always have options. I'm never stuck."

"That's where you're wrong." Desmond had his hand wrapped around Justina's neck so quick, even she didn't' realize she couldn't breathe until she started gasping for air. "You're my wife. I own you. I am your only option. So yes, you are stuck. Do you understand?" he eased up on his grip so she could respond.

"If I can't breathe, then neither can this baby."

"You seem to be breathing just fine to me. Now answer my question. Do you understand?"

"Perfectly."

"Excellent. It's important we're on the same page with everything in our marriage." Desmond's hand remained wrapped around Justina's neck but he was no longer applying pressure. At this point he didn't have to. He eyes and the lethal tone of his voice were doing enough damage.

"You better go. No need to keep Dominique waiting," Justina stated flatly.

It was at that very moment, Desmond realized how dangerous his wife was. Most women would be afraid if their husband had threatened and choked them up but she showed no signs of fear. Instead Justina's eyes were filled with defiance.

"I don't have to go," Desmond said, releasing

Justina's neck. "I'll stay here and let one of my men handle the Dominique situation. You and our baby clearly need me."

Desmond waited and searched for any sign of tenderness within Justina's soul and there it was. The rebelliousness disappeared and devotion was restored.

"Thank you." Justina sounded sincere but Desmond was under no delusion, it could switch at any moment. He knew he had married a cold and calculating woman but Desmond had genuinely fallen in love with Justina and he didn't want to lose her. It was clear to him, if he wanted to win her over and gain her loyalty and undying love, Justina had to be sure she would always come first. If not, her basic instinct was to go in survival mode and protect herself, which meant severing any emotional ties to him.

"Baby." Desmond reached out and held Justina's hand. "Please know you're my number one priority. No one will ever come before you."

"I want to believe you, Desmond but only time will tell." Justina let go of his hand and walked off before stopping and turning back to him. "However, I do appreciate the effort you just made, to assure me of your commitment to our marriage."

Chapter Seventeen

Going For Broke

"Dominique, thank goodness you okay. When our call went dead and I didn't hear from you, I got scared. Then by the time I got to the club, you were gone and wouldn't nobody tell me shit," Clarissa huffed.

"Sorry about that. I passed out when I heard you say Mrs. Armstrong was dead. She worked my nerves sometimes but I had a lot of love for her."

"Yeah, that shit fucked me up too. I still ain't over being the one to find Aspen murdered and now Mrs. Armstrong," Clarissa sighed. "I pray to never have to see another dead body again."

"I know it must fuck wit' you. Hearing Aspen get shot still rings in my head."

"So, where are you now, 'cause I know you ain't back at that condo."

"Nah. One of Desmond's men got me out the club and took me to see a doctor after I fainted. Once I was cleared to leave, he took me to a hotel. At first, we were waiting for Desmond but I guess something came up because he sent one of his men instead. They wouldn't let me make no calls or nothing for the first few days. Finally, they moved me to some house on the beach. It's really beautiful but it's out in the cut somewhere. They did give me a burner phone this morning, so of course I wanted to call and let you know I'm okay," Dominque explained.

"Dang, you must be sick of moving around."

"I am but I keep reminding myself that at least I'm alive. All I want is for Desmond to find Taren and get rid of her for good because I'm tired of having to watch my back. I wanna move on wit' my life. Speaking of Desmond, I just heard him come in. I'll call you back." Dominique quickly hung up the phone then checked her appearance in the mirror. Married or not, Dominique hadn't given up hope she would be the last chick standing and he would end up with her.

"How are you feeling?" Desmond asked when he walked in the den where Dominique was sitting.

"I'm better now that you're here."

"I stopped at that restaurant you like and got some of your favorites," he said handing her the to go bag.

"You're so sweet. Thank you. Any new leads on Taren?" Dominique questioned while taking the food out the bag, as she was starving.

"Not yet but if she's in Miami, I promise we will find her. Taren's not gonna make it outta here alive. I'm mad at myself for cancelling the security detail. If I kept them, Mrs. Armstrong would still be alive."

"Don't blame yourself. Taren is a psycho. People like that are capable of anything."

"You're right. The sooner we can erase her existence, the better off we'll all be, especially you. You were back dancing at the club and I could see that sparkle in your eyes again. You deserve some happiness, so I want this Taren situation resolved asap."

"I appreciate how much you care about me and my feelings. I guess that's why I was a little surprised you never showed up to the hotel after I spoke to you briefly and you said you were on the way."

"About that. Sammie will be your go to guy for now on. He's one of my best men. He'll make sure you get whatever you need."

"I don't understand. Are you saying Sammie will be the one checking up on me and to call him if I need anything?"

"Yes, that's what I'm saying."

"Why do I have to call Sammie and not you?" Dominique threw her food down, wanting to hear Desmond's response.

"I think it's for the best. I have a lot going on right now and Sammie will be able to dedicate more time to you."

"I get it." Dominique folded her arms with objection. "Your wife doesn't want you around me. Isn't that the real reason you passing me off to Sammie?"

"Yes, it has a lot to do with it," he admitted.

"Desmond, you don't need her. I can make

you so much happier," Dominique vowed, throwing caution out the window and making her intentions known.

"Dominique, you are beautiful and sweet. Any man would be lucky to have you but I'm not available."

"What is it...is it because she's some spoiled princess who grew up rich? I read all about her. I know who her father is." Dominique got up from the couch and went over to Desmond. She wanted him to see the passion in her eyes. "Justina doesn't deserve you. She's one of those privileged brats who thinks the whole world should revolve around her. She'll never appreciate you. Not like I do."

Dominique was going for broke. She leaned in and kissed Desmond. She wanted him to feel her soft lips against his. She was wearing a long, flowy slip dress and with just two simple moves, it was now on the floor. Dominique grabbed his hand and pressed it against her breasts so he could touch her hardened nipples. Desmond began caressing them, so she knew he was starting to give into temptation. Staying committed to her mission of making Desmond her man, she took his other hand and placed it inside her panties.

Dominique's pussy was dripping wet, causing him to get an immediate erection. From there it was a wrap. Once she saw them inches growing, she had his pants unzipped and his dick in her mouth, before he could even think about protesting. Her seduction game was strong and like most men, Desmond gave in.

Knowing this might be her last opportunity to reel Desmond in, Dominique wasn't holding back. She sucked his dick like she was a professional porno star. She could feel him trying to resist but her tongue action was too potent. After Desmond tried pulling away one last time, Dominique shut all that down, by sliding on top of the dick and riding it slow yet steady. She then played with her titties before leaning in and placing her nipple in his mouth. At this point, Desmond had been completely lured in and he was no longer fighting against it.

With each stroke, Dominique was relishing in finally making love to the man she so desired. She hated to play dirty to make it happen but when Desmond said he would no longer be coming around, Dominique made up her mind, she had to act fast. He was the only man she wanted and was willing to pull out all the stops to make him stay.

"I'm back!" Aaliyah sung into the phone.

"About time! It feels like you've been gone forever. How was your trip? I missed you," Angel said as she was driving on her way to work.

"I know, we were gone for almost a month but we had the most amazing time. Honestly, I could've stayed another few weeks but life calls. And I missed you too. Justina and I are getting together tomorrow for lunch and I wanted you to join us. What do you say?"

"I'll be there. Just let me know the time and place. I'm looking forward to it."

"Great! I'll text you later on with the info. Can't wait to see you and show all the beautiful pictures we took."

"I can't wait to see them and you! I'll be looking out for your text. Bye." Angel hung up with Aaliyah and immediately placed her next call. "Hey, you got that for me?"

"Give me a couple more days."

"I don't have a couple more days. My sister is back in town and I need the information now."

"There's a lot to go through. I'll have to work through the night."

"Then work through the night. I'll pay you triple, just get it done."

"Fine. I'll be in touch first thing in the morning and let you know what I have."

"Good, the earlier the better," Angel said, keeping her fingers cross she would hit pay dirt.

Taren had been twiddling her thumbs for the past week trying to figure out how she could get her last bit of revenge, before leaving Miami and disappearing, never to be heard from again.

"Man, there's got to be another way for me to get my hands on Dominique. But I have no fuckin' clue where Desmond has moved her and there have been no sightings of her at the strip club."

"You know what," Shayla said between puffs. "I was thinking," she continued, as Shayla thought she got her best ideas while smoking weed. "If Desmond is the one hiding Dominique, I doubt his wife could be happy about that. She pregnant too!" Shayla smacked.

"His wife is pregnant?" this was the first Taren heard.

"Yeah, I ran into her a couple days ago. Normally she be wearing all them fitted clothes, showing off that body," Shayla cracked making an hour glass shape with her hands. "But she had on some loose shit and I noticed that belly was poppin'. Homegirl saw me staring so she was quick to let me know she was pregnant and not gettin' fat," Shayla laughed.

"Okay, so Desmond's wife is pregnant and gettin' chubby, how the hell is that gon' help me get to Dominique?"

"Do I have to explain everythang...damn!" Shayla rolled her eyes, thinking she was the smart one out of the two. "If you pregnant and yo' husband is stashing one of his strippers, wouldn't you think they smashin'?! So, if I whisper a lil' something in the Mrs. ear, I bet she would lead us right to Dominique."

"Bitch, you brilliant! Why the fuck didn't I think of that," Taren shouted, throwing her hands in the air like her favorite football team just scored the winning touchdown.

"'Cause you ain't over here smokin' none of this good shit. I done told you, my brain be functioning to its fullest potential when I lighted up."

"Yeah, you do be saying that shit," Taren agreed. "Okay, so when you gone whisper them lies in the wife's ear?"

"Who said it was a lie?! We both know niggas ain't shit. He got his trophy wife Justina at home and in the office and the stripper stashed away. Sounds 'bout right to me."

"Man, I don't give a fuck if he sexing Dominique or not, as long as you make Justina think he is!" Taren exclaimed.

"Let me handle, Justina. I know her type. Once I throw out a few trigger words, she'll be pushin' a hundred on the highway to snatch Dominique up. Just make sure you stay on that ass, 'cause she gon' be driving fast," Shayla winked.

Chapter Eighteen

What Had Happened Was...

"Good morning," Justina smiled, taking off her negligee to get in the shower.

"Wow, look at you. Your stomach seemed to grow overnight," Desmond said, placing his hand on her protruding belly. "You're beautiful." Desmond stroked her long hair, thinking to himself

Justina now had the pregnancy glow.

"I don't feel beautiful. I feel fat but I'm loving the thickness and rapid speed my hair is growing," she giggled. "So where were you yesterday? You got in so late," she asked casually.

"I went to see Dominique."

"Excuse me?" Instead of getting in the shower, Justina grabbed a towel and wrapped it around her body ready to cuss Desmond out. "Why the fuck did you go see her?"

"Baby, calm down, it's not what you think. I wanted to let Dominique know Sammie would be her point person for now on. That she could no longer call me because my wife comes first." Desmond caressed the side of Justina's face and gazed lovingly in her eyes as if he was telling her the absolute truth. Which he was, he just left out the part, that he fucked the shit out of her in the midst of all that.

"You must think I'm a fool!" Justina yelled, pushing Desmond's hand away from her. "You could've told Dominique that shit over the phone. Are you fuckin' her? You better tell me the truth now or live to regret it later," she warned.

"No! I'm sharing this with you because I want you to understand how committed I am to our marriage," Desmond implored. "I felt I should tell Dominique in person, that besides her working at the strip club, I wasn't having any other dealings with her. And once I handled the Taren situation, she had to move back to her own place. I swear," he continued.

"Baby, she's staying at my beach house in Key, Biscayne. The one I took you to. You can call and ask her or better yet, go talk to her in person." Of course, Desmond was praying Justina wouldn't do either but he felt it sounded much more believable, if he sprinkled bits of the truth instead of spreading all lies.

"Get Dominique on the phone," Justina stated, calling Desmond's bluff. But like any halfway seasoned poker player, he started dialing the number as if the truth was on his side.

"No problem. I'm calling her now." Desmond had connections with the most ruthless criminals from coming up in the streets. Negotiated deals with some of the shadiest motherfuckers when conducting business but under the most stressful situations, never did he think, he might break a sweat, until now. When he came up with the idea of coming clean with Justina, this wasn't how he imagined it playing out.

"Is the phone ringing?" Justina wanted to know.

"Yeah, it's ringing."

"Okay, hand it to me."

As bad as Desmond wanted to say hell no. He did what his wife asked. He placed the phone in Justina's hand.

"Whatever that thing was, you had with Dominique. It better be over," Justina made clear, then ending the call and handing the phone back to her husband. "I don't want to hear that woman's name again."

"I promise you won't. Dominique will never be an issue again."

Desmond watched while Justina took her shower, thinking how close he came to having things blow up in his face. As great as the sex was with Dominique, he regretted letting it happen. There was no denying he always had a soft spot for her but she didn't make his heart race like Justina did. There was this thrill factor Desmond got from being with a woman so complicated. It was like trying to tame the wildest animal in the jungle and right when you felt you had it mastered, you uncover another layer needing to be trained. Desmond was in love and infatuated with Justina and there was nothing anyone could do to change that.

Dale was standing on the bedroom terrace, staring out at the breathtaking ocean views.

"When I get back we should take a dip," Aaliyah suggested, walking up behind her husband and seeing how enticing the infinity pool looked.

"Only if we get in there naked," Dale smiled.

"We can do that, especially since I can't fit into any of my bathing suits with this growing tummy."

"I love seeing your stomach grow. It means my son is getting stronger and stronger."

"Or your daughter!" Aaliyah slapped Dale on the arm. "I would love to have a little you running around though."

"Yeah, because I don't think the world is ready for another Aaliyah. Luckily, I have the one and only version," Dale said lovingly, pulling his wife close in his arms.

"Did I tell you how much I love you?"

"Not since this morning, so it's time for you to tell me again."

"I love you, Dale Clayborn."

"I love you too, Mrs. Aaliyah Clayborn."

"Say it one more time. I never get tired of hearing the sound to that," she blushed.

"I love you too, Mrs. Aaliyah Clayborn. The most beautiful woman in the world." The newlyweds embraced in a lingering kiss.

"You're not going anywhere are you because I want us to continue this after I get back from having lunch with Justina and Angel."

"I'll be right here. I'm waiting for the technician to arrive. For some reason, the security cameras aren't working."

"Okay, well I shouldn't be gone long. Hopefully the technician would've came and left too by the time I return, so we can have the house all to ourselves," Aaliyah teased. "Call if you want me to bring you anything back," she said waving goodbye. "I love you."

"Love you more." Dale pressed his lips against his two fingers before turning them towards his wife. Aaliyah then blew a kiss back to her husband and Dale caught it. It was a gesture of love between them that they always shared.

Shayla had been anxiously waiting all morning for Justina's arrival to work. She was beginning to think she would be a no show until noticing her drop top white Bentley pull up in the parking lot. Shayla scrambled to get out the car and head towards the entrance before Justina had a chance to see her. Shayla went over what she was going to say one more time as Justina was walking in her direction. She pretended to be searching for something in her purse but made sure to position herself where Justina had to cross her path.

"Hey Shayla," Justina called out without missing a step. Her strut was so swift, Shayla had to react fast before she got through the doors.

"Justina! Can you hold up a minute!" she yelled, putting her hand up to make sure she got her attention.

"What is it? I'm already starting my day later than planned, so I only have a second to spare." Justina wasted no time getting to the point so Shayla did the same.

"I respect you a lot. For one, you a bad bitch

and two, I wouldn't have this well paying gig, if it won't for you."

Justina gave Shayla a blank stare like she had heard all this before and unless she had something new to add, get out her way. "Okay."

"So, it really bothered me when this friend of mine who is cool wit' this chick named Clarissa said her friend Dominique was fuckin' around wit' yo' husband." That was a mouthful but Shayla wanted to make sure she got it all out and it worked. She didn't have it before but Shayla had Justina's full attention now.

"Back up a minute. How do you know it's my husband?"

"Well what had happened was the girl Clarissa said, Dominique was fuckin' around wit' the man who owned this strip club and was part owner of Angel's Girls. I overheard Elsa saying you were married to Angel's business partner, so I assumed my friend had to be talkin' 'bout yo' man. My bad!" Shayla put her hands up as if being apologetic. "I call myself tryna look out for you, 'cause a nigga got to be crazy to fuck around on you but clearly it ain't yo' husband. I must've got the men mixed up," Shayla said walking off.

"Wait!" This time it was Justina yelling out,

desperate to get Shayla's attention. "Tell me what your friend told you again."

Shayla went through the whole spill again, this time dabbling a little extra here and there to get Justina completely vexed. The shit was sounding like some true sipping hot tea, Shayla started believing the story she supposedly conjured up was true. By the time she was done listening, Justina had murdered and buried both Dominique's and Desmond's bodies at least twice.

"Where you going?!" Shayla shouted as if she was clueless, when Justina stormed off but got no response. She patted herself on the back when she saw Taren exit out the parking lot, right on Justina's ass.

"Elsa, has Justina come in yet?" Angel questioned after passing by her office and not seeing her.

"No, not yet. Do you want me to let you know when she comes in?"

"That's okay. I have to head out but I'll be seeing her later on for lunch."

"You and Justina are having lunch...is it

snowing outside?" Elsa stood up and looked out the window jokingly.

"Funny. My sister is back in town and as I told you, her and Justina are besties. The three of us are having lunch today, so she can tell us about her trip. I guess we have one thing in common, our love for Aaliyah."

"How special." Elsa gave a cynical smile.

"I have to make a stop before our lunch, so I may or may not be in for the rest of the day. As always, I'm counting on you to hold things down."

Angel headed to her car, having no idea only a few minutes ago, Taren, a woman she once considered a best friend had been parked a few feet away. Desmond had informed her, the former friend she now considered an enemy, was spotted in Miami and more than likely killed the woman he hired to look after Dominique. But Angel wasn't worried. She kept a gun in her purse and both cars. Plus, she didn't think Taren had the guts to approach her face to face. Regardless, Angel would handle the situation if and when it became a problem. At the moment, she had more pressing issues to deal with.

Chapter Nineteen

No More Lies

"Mrs. Blackwell, what are you doing here?" one of the men hired to protect Dominique asked when Justina pulled up with guns blazing. No, she wasn't literally carrying any weapons but Justina's walk was so mean, she was spitting bullets.

"Get out of my way. I came here to speak to Dominique. If you have a problem with that, call my husband. Now move!"

Both men stepped to the side and let Justina through. She followed the scent of cheap perfume to a bedroom in the back of the beach house, where she found Dominique lounging in the plush king size bed, like this was her crib and she was the queen of this shit.

"Get the fuck up." Justina demanded.

Dominque was shocked to see the woman she detested standing in the doorway. "What are doing here?"

"I own this house since Desmond is my husband. What's your fuckin' excuse?"

"I was brought here by your husband because he wants to make sure I'm well taken care of."

"Spoken like a true low budget hoe."

"I'm not a hoe. Desmond cares about me."

"I see. Do tell, Dominique. I would love to hear all about your relationship with my husband."

Dominique was salivating at the mouth, ready to share every explicit detail about how her husband's dick tasted in her mouth and felt inside her pussy.

"I'll be more than happy to tell you." As the

words were about to spill out of Dominique's mouth, her burner phone started ringing. "Hello."

"I know my wife is there with you and you better not tell her a thing, are we clear, Dominique?"

"Yes."

"Put her on the phone." Dominique handed the phone to Justina.

"What the fuck do you want, Desmond?" the fury in Justina's voice had him on edge.

"Baby, why are you there?" he kept his tone even and calm. "I thought we resolved everything this morning."

"I thought so too until Clarissa started running her mouth, telling people her friend Dominique was fuckin' my husband."

"That's a lie! Clarissa never said that!" Dominique jumped out the bed, defending her friend.

"Who is Clarissa?" Desmond questioned, trying to stall until he could come up with the right words to calm Justina down.

"Oh, now you don't know who Clarissa is? That's funny since Dominique evidently does."

"Yeah, she's one of the dancers at the club. I don't know why she would be saying some shit like that. Dominique and I don't have that type of relationship. I already explained this to you."

"Right before you called, I think Dominique was about to tell me the exact opposite. Isn't that right, Dominique. She was telling me how much you care about her."

"Baby, listen..."

"Don't call me baby. I told you to tell me the truth this morning but instead you lied to my face. I'm done with you."

"Justina, you don't mean that. You're my fuckin' wife!"

"Not for long. I'm almost positive Amir would be willing to take me back, especially under the circumstances. You can have this bargain basement hussy. I'm going back to New York."

"You want him so bad, Dominique. Well, he's all yours," Justina scoffed, tossing the phone back to her.

"What the fuck did you tell Clarissa!" Desmond roared.

"Nothing," Dominique said nervously. She had never heard Desmond sound so upset. It was freaking her out.

"You stay in that room and don't you say another word to my wife." Desmond then called back the worker who had informed him Justina was there.

"What's up boss."

"Is my wife still there?"

"She's getting in her car now."

"Don't let her leave. I don't care what you have to do. I'm headed to you now. I'll see you shortly."

From a short distance, Taren watched what appeared to be two bodyguards having an intense conversation with Justina. She was clearly trying to leave but they were making it impossible for her to do so. "Damn, she feisty," Taren laughed, observing Justina cursing them out. At one point, she picked up a huge rock and threw it at one of the men. It barely missed him and only because he ducked down. But it did smash one of the front windows. Justina seemed unfazed. "Who knew rich bitches had all that toughness," Taren said shaking her head.

She had become so caught up in all the commotion, Taren was about to let a window of opportunity slip through her fingers. *I've only seen two men at the house and I doubt there are any inside, if so I think they would've come outside by now to assist these knuckleheads because they damn sure need it. They letting a pregnant woman run them in circles,* Taren thought to herself.

She decided it was time to make her move. Taren pulled her car around, so it was facing the back of the house. She could see a door on the side that you could get to from the beach. Taren grabbed both her guns, pulled down her hat and put on her sunglasses before heading towards the house. She could still hear all the yelling and chaos at the front of the house, so she knew everyone was currently occupied. When Taren got to the side door she had a clear view of the inside since it was an open floorplan. She could see a slight glimpse of what appeared to be Dominique looking outside at Justina and the two men. Taren tried to open the side door but it was locked. It was too close in proximity to break the glass because Dominique would probably hear it. Instead, Taren ran around to the back of the house. She was about to break the glass on that door but to her delight it was unlocked.

Bingo, she thought as she cracked open the door and slid inside. Through a large mirror on the wall, Taren could see Dominique standing in the same spot enthralled in the mayhem outside just like she had been a few minutes earlier. Justina was a firecracker, so Taren got why Dominique couldn't peel her eyes away. It also worked in her favor. She made a pit stop in the kitchen and grabbed the heaviest pan she could find. Taren walked softly but because the noise outside was unbelievably loud, Dominique didn't suspect a thing until the all-clad stainless steel pan connected to the back of her head, knocking Dominique out cold.

By the time anyone noticed, Taren had dragged Dominique's petite body out the house and dumped her in the trunk of her car. She had one down and one more to go. Taren finally believed things were working in her favor.

After a long fought battle, Justina finally managed to drive off before Desmond arrived. She almost had to run over both of his workers to do so but eventually they decided they rather get cursed out by their boss than end up dead, so they let Justina leave. She was rushing upstairs to pack up her belongings before Desmond got home, when she heard the doorbell ring.

"Who the hell could that be," she said out loud deciding to ignore it until whoever it was started banging on the door. Justina went to the door and saw it was Aaliyah. "Hey! I'm so sorry. I totally missed our lunch date. If you only knew what sort of day I had," Justina complained, letting her inside.

"Oh really?" Aaliyah said, unable to take her eyes off Justina's stomach. "You're not nearly as far along as me but your stomach is the same size as mine. That must be a big baby you're carrying."

"Oh yeah, my appetite has been off the charts. My doctor told me I need to slow down," Justina lied. "So, how was the lunch? I was really looking forward to coming and hearing about your trip, the wedding and all the beautiful pictures I'm sure you took."

"I was disappointed you didn't show up too. Luckily, Angel was there to keep me company. We had lots to discuss."

"I'm sure you did." Justina smiled, keeping the conversation light and brief. She wanted to get out the house before Desmond arrived but she wasn't in the mood to go into details with Aaliyah about all the drama that went down. She was trying to figure out the quickest way to get her best friend to leave without raising any red flags. "Aaliyah, I hate to ask you to leave but..."

"I'm not going anywhere, Justina and neither are you."

"Is there something wrong? Your demeanor changed in a matter of seconds."

"On my way over here, I had everything I was going to say and do mapped out. But then you open the door and I see this huge belly and the realization that you're pregnant, kicks in."

"You're all over the place right now. What exactly are you trying to tell me?"

"It was you. You're the one who had Nesa tell Dale about my father killing his brother."

"Aaliyah, what are you talking about? That's absurd. I had no idea Supreme killed Emory."

"I don't know how you found out but you did! You deceitful, evil bitch!" Aaliyah screamed, ready to claw the skin right off Justina's face.

"Okay, Aaliyah you need to relax. Come have a seat and calm down."

"Don't patronize me. I knew me and Amir hurt you but never did I fathom it turned you into a complete monster. My father and entire family could've been killed and I almost lost the man that I love because of your twisted idea of revenge. But that was your plan, right. To turn Dale against me so I could be as miserable as you." Aaliyah was so enraged she was on the verge of tears. Every bone in her body wanted to beat the living shit out of Justina. But it was impossible for her to do, knowing Justina was carrying a child and she was too.

"I don't know where all this is coming from but it's nothing but lies. I'm guessing Angel is filling your head with this nonsense. You know how much she hates me. Why are you even listening to her?"

"Amazing how easy it is for you to tell me one lie after another. It makes me wonder how many more secrets you've been keeping from me. But you're right, Angel does hate you but that's because she could see the truth when I couldn't."

"So, you're just going to take the word of a sister you barely know over your best friend?"

"It's funny, Angel figured I would side with you. But my sister is no dummy. I had so much going on that I asked her to get the Boss Babe poster I got for you framed. Unbeknownst to me, she had a camera installed in it. After hiring someone to go through hours of video, they finally came across a heartfelt confession you made to your husband."

Justina could do many things but rewriting facts wasn't one of them. There was no disputing the truth, especially when it was caught on tape. The only thing left for Justina to do was beg Aaliyah for forgiveness and hope she had mercy on her. The thing was, Justina wasn't in the mood to beg. Her mind was elsewhere. She was stuck on the altercation she had with Dominique and at this moment how much she loathed Desmond. Her focus was on getting out his house, not saving her friendship with Aaliyah.

"There's no excuse for what I did. When we were at the hospital and I told you and Amir how deeply both of you hurt me and then you apologized, I instantly regretted having Nesa tell Dale what I knew but by then it was too late. The damage was done. I was relieved when you and Dale were able to reconcile. It was the only thing that eased some of my guilt. I know you may never forgive me but I'm truly sorry for all the pain I caused you and your family."

"If your mouth is moving a bunch of lies are surly being told. I don't believe anything you say. You're sick just like your mother."

"Aaliyah, I think you should go now before we say things that we'll both regret."

"Please, there's nothing I can say to you that I'll regret. I can't stomp and drag you through this house because beating the shit out of a pregnant woman, just isn't dignified but trust, you have an ass whooping coming. Until then, I'm going to do everything in my power, to make sure you pay in other ways. What you had Nesa do isn't a crime but murder is."

"Excuse me! Aaliyah, you need to get out now!" Justina screamed.

"I'll leave but I know you murdered Nesa, thinking your secret would die with her but it didn't. Angel and I are going to find the proof we need to put yo' trifling ass behind bars for the rest of your pathetic life. I put that on everything!" Aaliyah swore on her way out, slamming the door so hard, the house shook.

Chapter Twenty

The Smell Of Death

"I should've at least punched her one good time!" Aaliyah yelled, pounding her fist on the steering wheel, as she was driving home. "I can't believe Justina could do something this cruel."

Aaliyah shook her head still in disbelief, pulling up in the driveway. She was itching to tell Dale what Justina had done, hoping he'd be so pissed, he would step in and try to convince

Desmond to divorce Justina's evil ass.

I don't understand how Desmond can be married to a woman who is capable of being that cold hearted. She doesn't deserve a husband or that baby she's carrying, Aaliyah thought to herself while opening the front door. "Dale! Dale!" she called out the second her heels hit the marble foyer. "He's probably upstairs," Aaliyah mumbled taking a few more steps.

Once Aaliyah turned right towards the entrance of the wrap around spiral stairs, she was hit with the most excruciating pain in the lower part of her abdomen. Then she began to vomit. Her body reacting to what she was seeing. Dale's throat had been slit from ear to ear. He was face up with his body slumped back on the bottom stairs, eyes wide open as if he had died in complete shock. He had also been shot twice in the chest.

Initially, Aaliyah couldn't even speak. She became dizzy and the room seemed to be spinning. Before passing out she managed to dial 911, begging for help.

Dominique came too, tied to a chair and duct tape covering her mouth, wrist and ankles. An extra length of rope was placed around her stomach area and between the arms to secure her firmly and prevent her from trying to get up or squirming too much.

"You finally woke the fuck up," Taren grumbled putting out her cigarette on the table. "Sheesh, it took you long enough. Now listen, I'ma take this tape off yo' mouth, if you yell, you see these pliers," Taren held them up. "I will pull off a toenail, one at a time," she smirked. "Sounds horrible, right?! I saw it in some Netflix movie I was watching. So, no screaming,"

Taren ripped off the tape from Dominique's mouth. "Ouch!" she shrieked.

"Stop actin' like such a baby," Taren taunted, sitting down in the chair next to Dominique. "Now listen, I'm short on time so we have to hurry this up."

"Why are you doing this to me? I haven't talked to the police. I'm not gonna turn you in?"

"Fuck the police, you told Desmond. That's even worse. But I'm not worried about him right now. I need you for bait."

"Bait?" Dominique frowned.

"Yes, so I can get the real prize...Angel. You know she's the one responsible for killing my father."

"I didn't know that," Dominique said timidly.

"Yep. It's time for Angel to be held accountable for what she did and you are gonna help me."

"But I don't even know Angel like that. She wouldn't come help me."

"Well you better hope she does, or you're dead," Taren laughed. "Besides, people seem to love saving you. Both Desmond and Angel already tried. I guess because you so little and cute. You seem so harmless. But I have a pretty good feeling, you have no problem pulling out all the stops when it's time to go after something you want. Am I right?" Taren goaded.

"I don't know what you mean," Dominique said coyly.

"Don't be shy. You don't have to pretend to be that sweet, innocent girl with me. I don't wanna save you. But it works great on people like Desmond and Angel. But since Desmond is currently preoccupied with his wife, then the only person left to help you is Angel."

"I really don't feel comfortable with this." Dominique's eyes teared up.

"No crying, Dominque! Now you have to put yo' big girl panties on. You have to decide right now. Do you want to live or die? Answer me!" Taren barked.

"I want to live," Dominique sobbed.

"That's my girl. Now here," Taren put a piece of paper in Dominique's lap. "This is what I want you to say to Angel. Don't fuck it up or I'll have to use these pliers on those cute little toes." Taren had the creepiest grin on her face which made Dominique cringe. She didn't want to set Angel up but she also didn't want to experience a slow and painful death at the hands of a psycho.

Besides, Dominique knew Taren was absolutely right about one thing. At the moment, Desmond's only concern was Justina. She wasn't even sure he knew or even cared she was gone. There was only one person who might be able to keep her alive and Dominique was praying Angel would come through.

"Get your hands off of me!" Justina hollered, before smacking the shit out of Desmond.

Desmond stopped for a minute, pressed his

hand on his mouth and saw he was bleeding. He wasn't surprised because Justina struck him with the hand she wore her enormous wedding ring on. He was tempted to lunge at his wife but Desmond didn't want her to fall down the stairs and harm the baby. Instead he ran after her.

"Justina, get back here!" he barked chasing her to their bedroom. "You need to listen to me," he pleaded.

"I heard all your lies. Now stay away from me. This marriage is over!"

Desmond took a deep breath, so he could calm himself down. Both of them were being driven by rage and somebody had to take a step back or things would quickly go from bad to worse.

"I don't want you to go. I don't want a divorce. You're my wife and I love you."

"If you love me, you wouldn't stand in my face and lie over and over again. I shared my deepest and darkest secrets with you. You, sonofabitch!" Justina roared, throwing an expensive vase Desmond had gotten on a trip to Rome. He watched it break into tiny little pieces. She then grabbed another vase ready to throw that too but she was hoping this one made contact with Desmond's head.

"You're absolutely right and I was wrong to lie to you. I'm not having an affair with Dominique but I did have sex with her once," Desmond admitted. "I gave into temptation and I regret it. Baby, I'm so, so sorry. But I swear it was only one time."

Justina's once heavy breathing seemed to cool down. For some reason, she believed this particular admission, unlike the other times but maybe because Desmond was actually telling the truth. She put the vase down and sat on the bed. Desmond came towards her.

"Don't touch me," she said putting her hand up.

"Justina, I lied before but this is the truth. It only happened once but I swear it will never happen again. I can't lose you and I damn sure ain't gon' let you run back to Amir. You don't love him, you love me."

"I was what you call a late bloomer. Even when I look at myself now, the reflection of the young me is what I see a lot of times. But I already shared my insecurities with you. You know Amir cheating with Aaliyah almost destroyed me. Then you turn around and do the exact same thing."

"I'm not excusing what I did. In a lot of ways

what I did is even worse because I'm your husband. But I think what cut you so deep with Amir,
is he cheated with your best friend."

"Oh, so I should be relieved you had sex with
a woman I can't stand."

"No. All I'm saying is Dominique isn't a part
of your life and she's not a part of mine anymore.
You'll never have to see her again, so there won't
be a reminder of my infidelity."

"It's not that easy." Justina got off the bed and
walked towards the double glass doors leading
outside to the terrace. "I need to be able to trust
you."

"You can. I made a horrible mistake. I
should've never let myself get in a position where
something like that could happen. Dominique
will no longer be working at the club and whatever else I have to do to prove my loyalty to you, I
will. I want to save our marriage. Please, Justina,
don't give up on us," Desmond pleaded.

"Okay but you better not ever hurt me
again...ever."

"I will never hurt you again," he promised.

Desmond held onto Justina tightly. His
strong arms wrapped around her, did give Justina the sense of security she desperately needed.

With Aaliyah knowing the truth, their relationship was over. The only person Justina felt she had was Desmond and the baby growing inside her.

"Answer your fuckin' phone, Desmond!" Angel screamed but he wasn't answering. After Dominique called begging to get picked up because she was afraid someone was following her, Angel immediately reached out to Desmond. He was adamant that he would protect Dominique so Angel wanted to find out what was going on.

Angel kept driving to the address Dominique said to pick her up at. She sounded scared and vulnerable. All Angel kept thinking about, was when she found her knocked out, lying next to the bomb Taren had detonated. Then when Dominique begged her not to leave her side, as the club was falling apart around them but she left to go save Aaliyah and Justina. Angel harbored a lot of guilt, thinking she should've done more for Dominique because she had been through so much at the hands of Taren. She figured being there for Dominique in her time of need would ease some of that guilt.

When Angel pulled up to the street, she could see a shadowy figure but wasn't sure who it was. She also had no way of calling Dominique because before they hung up, she said the battery on her phone was about to die any second. As Angel was proceeding slowly ahead, the shadowy figure began waving their arm and then coming towards her. When they got closer, she immediately recognized Dominque's face.

"Hey!" Angel said rolling down the window. "Get in," she unlocked the doors.

"Thank you so much for coming to get me," Dominique said, getting in the backseat. "Please forgive me for..." before she could finish her sentence, Taren had sneaked up to the side of the car and jumped in the front, with one gun aimed at Angel's head and the other at Dominique.

"Don't even think about it, Angel. All I have to do is pull the trigger and you're dead."

"Taren, you don't wanna do this," Angel sighed.

"Oh, yes I do."

"Please don't kill me!" Dominique cried.

"Shut up with all that whining!" Taren roared. She took the gun aimed at Dominique and smashed her over the head with it. "Thank goodness I don't have to hear her mouth. That should keep her silent for the next couple of hours but by then she'll be dead. The only reason I didn't go ahead and shoot her now, is because after I kill the both of you, I'm taking your car. And I don't wanna drive a long distance with all her blood in the backseat."

"I can't believe I never saw how insane you are. You're really sick," Angel gasped, disturbed by Taren's actions.

"Shut up and drive," Taren ordered, pressing the muzzle of the gun on the side of Angel's head. "Turn right at the next light," she said. "Do what I say and I'll make your death quick. If you try and get cute, I'ma have you beggin' me to end yo' life, so the pain can stop."

"Taren, you're never going to get away with this. Forget about the police, my father will hunt you down and kill you."

"Yo' father! Fuck yo' daddy!" Taren hit Angel with the gun. Not hard enough to knock her out like she did Dominique but enough to bring sufficient pain. "You the reason I ain't got my daddy now. You think I give a fuck 'bout yours."

"I can't believe you still blame me for what

happened to your dad," Angel said, wiping away the blood trickling down the side of her face, from being hit with the gun.

"It is your fault! And you think you so fuckin' great 'cause Nico Carter yo' daddy and you got yo'self a dumbass sister. Fuck you and yo' family." Taren had gotten herself completely riled up. She was rambling on in the car like a deranged woman.

Taren is certifiable. There is no way I'm following her directions because I'm not about to drive myself to the scene of my own grave. If I'm going to make a move, I have to do it now. I rather die in a car crash then let myself be murdered by this crazy bitch, Angel said to herself. It's now or never.

"FUUUUUUCK! There's a dead body in the street!" Angel screamed so loud Taren couldn't help but turn in the direction she was pointing. With Angel's outburst being spontaneous, it gave credence she was telling the truth. While Taren was distracted, she then slammed down on the brake, causing the rear wheels to lock. They stopped turning and began skidding. Then another car slammed into them from behind and Angel's Benz started spinning. The car rolled over the pavement/sidewalk, grassy verge, across a ditch, curved a 5-foot stone wall before coming to a rest in a field. The car was totaled and everyone was bruised up. Dominique and Taren got it the worst because neither had on their seatbelts.

Angel looked around to see if she could spot one of the guns Taren had been holding but everything was so dark, she could barely see a thing. She always kept a gun in the glove department but due to the damage in the front of the car, it was completely smashed in and her purse, where she kept another gun, was also missing.

"I have to get outta here," Angel mumbled trying to squeeze through the broken glass window. When she finally escaped, her next objective was to pull Dominique out the back. Her petite frame was making it a lot easier for Angel to maneuver her body out.

"Where the fuck you think you going!" Taren had slid up on Angel like the snake she is and grabbed her by the back of her hair, yanking Angel to the ground. Taren threw her body on top of Angel and started punching her over and over again. Taren had all this pent-up anger and aggression that she was finally able to release on the woman she blamed for her father's death.

Angel could feel a stick by her hand, so she grabbed on to it and swung it over Taren's head. It didn't do any damage but it did give Angel a chance to dig her nails in Taren's face. She squeezed down with all her strength, causing Taren to roll off her. One shoe had come off during the car accident so Angel took off the other and used the pointy heel to pounce Taren on every part of her body. Then she started stomping her with her foot and Taren grabbed her leg causing Angel to fall face down. While lying on the ground, she noticed her purse was beside the back tire. Right as Taren stood up, she ran towards her purse and she could feel Taren catching up to her. Angel flung open her purse, grabbed her gun, cocked it and lit Taren's body up, until she had no more bullets left.

"Finally, that crazy heifa is dead!" Angel rejoiced, falling to the ground.

Chapter Twenty-One

A Baby Is Born

"Mommy! I'm so glad you're here. I had the most horrible nightmare." Aaliyah lifted her arms up and Precious came rushing over to comfort her daughter.

"It's okay, Aaliyah. I'm here for you." Precious rubbed her back, wanting to soothe her agony.

"Mommy, it seemed so real. I mean one minute I was walking through the door and the next

I see all this blood. Oh gosh, I need to speak to Dale and tell him what happened." Aaliyah was talking nonstop at an insanely rapid speed. She had been going in and out like this for the last week. It broke Precious's heart.

"Baby, it's okay. Get some rest. We can talk about it later."

"I don't want to talk about it later. I want to talk about it now. I need to get up and eat," Aaliyah said, yanking the blanket off her. "I know my baby must be hungry," she muttered patting her stomach.

"Aaliyah, lay back down."

"Mommy, why are all these tubes in my arms?" Aaliyah looked down at her arms, her stomach and then she stared back up at her mother. As if ready and mentally strong enough to face the truth, Aaliyah cried her heart out.

"I'm so sorry," Precious kept saying over again. "But we will get through this."

"Why me! Why me!" Aaliyah wailed. "My husband is dead and our baby too," she wept, touching her now flat tummy. "I have nothing to live for."

"That's not true. Don't say such things. I remember when I lost the baby Supreme and I were supposed to have. I felt like I had died too but then God gave me you." Precious caressed her daughter's face. She could see the once shining light within her going dim. "I know you don't believe this right now but one day you will fall in love again and you will become a mother. This is not the end for you, Aaliyah."

"I can't stay here in Miami. It's too painful. This is the place my husband was murdered and I miscarried our baby. Love doesn't live here anymore. I feel nothing but hate and rage."

"You don't have to stay here. I'm taking you home to New York where you belong." Precious held Aaliyah's hand, determined to heal her daughter's broken heart.

Five Months Later...

"Look how beautiful my son is," Desmond stated proudly. Standing in the custom nursery he designed, holding the newborn he named after himself.

"He is pretty perfect," Justina smiled.

"Yes, just like his mother." Desmond kissed his wife. "Thank you for blessing me with this precious boy."

"I guess I finally did something right in my life. Falling in love with you and giving birth to a healthy, beautiful baby."

"You left out boy. Beautiful baby boy," Desmond boasted. He never made it a secret his preference was a boy but Justina had no idea how important it was to him until their son was born. He never even questioned the paternity. In Desmond's eyes this was his son and nothing would change that.

"Baby, do you really have to go out of town tonight. I hate being in this house without you," Justina said.

"I know but I'll only be gone for a couple days. I've already postponed the trip twice because I wanted to be here with you and our son but I have to get this deal closed. I'm coming right back." Desmond leaned over and kissed Justina before putting the baby back in his crib.

"Please hurry back. My life isn't the same when you're not here."

"Of course, it isn't because I am your life." Desmond believed those words he spoke to be true and after initially fighting against it, Justina did too. Desmond found a way to do exactly what he always intended, break Justina down until she was emotionally and mentally dependent on him. A lot of that had to do with her friendship with Aaliyah ending. Justina began to feel vulnerable and alone. She isolated herself and Desmond became her lifeline and that's exactly the way he wanted it.

After Desmond left to catch his flight, Justina nursed her son before falling asleep on one of the couches downstairs. Her peaceful rest was interrupted, when a heavy breeze seemed to jolt through the house.

"Why does it feel like the wind is blowing in here?" Justina sputtered out loud, waking up from her sleep. "Did I leave a window open," she wondered, getting up to walk around and check. Then she froze for a second when she saw the front door wide open. She ran to shut it and make sure it was locked.

I know I was exhausted but there is no way I would've left the front door open. I'm positive I closed it when I kissed Desmond goodbye, Justina thought to herself as she headed upstairs to check on her son.

When Justina was walking down the long hallway, the first thing she noticed was her son's door was closed. She always kept it open to make sure she never missed a sound he might make. Justina put her hand on the doorknob and turned it slowly, knowing she didn't want to see what was waiting for her on the other side of the door. She took slow steps towards his crib, dreading what would come next. Justina's piercing scream echoed throughout the house and could probably be heard in every multi-million-dollar mansion in their exclusive neighborhood.

"Hush little baby don't say a word..." Aaliyah stopped in the middle of singing the nursery rhyme and held the newborn baby close to her. "Are you smiling at me? You little cutie," she cooed, leaning back in the rocking chair. "Justina has a husband and a child, everything that was supposed to be mine. She doesn't deserve a beautiful baby boy like you. But no worries, all that has now changed. Your mommy will soon find out, how agonizing it is, when the one you love the most, is ripped out of your life forever." Aaliyah smiled, pleased with herself, for being the one to bring Justina the worst pain yet.

Read The Entire Bitch Series in This Order

Coming Soon

A KING PRODUCTION

Stackin' PAPER

a novel

JOY DEJA KING

Chapter One
A Killer Is Born

Philly, 1993

"Please, Daquan, don't hit me again!" the young mother screamed, covering her face in defense mode. She hurriedly pushed herself away from her predator, sliding her body on the cold hardwood floor.

"Bitch, get yo' ass back over here!" he barked, grabbing her matted black hair and dragging her into the kitchen. He reached for the hot skillet from the top of the oven, and you could hear the oil popping underneath the fried chicken his wife had been cooking right before he came home. "Didn't I tell you to have my food ready on the table when I came home?"

"I… I… I was almost finished, but you came home early," Teresa stuttered, "Ouch!" she yelled as her neck damn near snapped when Daquan gripped her hair even tighter.

"I don't want to hear your fuckin' excuses. That's what yo' problem is. You so damn hard headed and neva want to listen. But like they say, a hard head make fo' a soft ass. You gon' learn to listen to me."

"Please, please, Daquan, don't do this! Let me finish frying your chicken and I'll never do this again. Your food will be ready and on the table everyday on time. I promise!"

"I'm tired of hearing your damn excuses."

"*Bang!*" was all you heard as the hot skillet came crashing down on Teresa's head. The hot oil splashed up in the air, and if Daquan hadn't moved forward and turned his head, his face would've been saturated with the grease.

But Teresa wasn't so lucky, as the burning oil grazed her hands, as they were protecting her face and part of her thigh.

After belting out in pain from the grease, she then noticed blood trickling down from the open gash on the side of her forehead. But it didn't stop there. Daquan then put the skillet down and began kicking Teresa in her ribs and back like she was a diseased infected dog that had just bitten him.

"Yo', Pops, leave moms alone! Why you always got to do this? It ain't never no peace when you come in this house." Genesis stood in the kitchen entrance with his fists clenched and panting like a bull. He had grown sick and tired of watching his father beat his mother down almost every single day. At the age of eleven he had seen his mother receive more ass whippings than hugs or any indication of love.

"Boy, who the fuck you talkin' to? You betta get yo' ass back in your room and stay the hell outta of grown people's business."

"Genesis, listen to your father. I'll be alright. Now go

back to your room," his mother pleaded.

Genesis just stood there unable to move, watching his mother and feeling helpless. The blood was now covering her white nightgown and she was covering her midsection, obviously in pain trying to protect the baby that was growing inside of her. He was in a trance, not knowing what to do to make the madness stop. But he was quickly brought back to reality when he felt his jaw almost crack from the punch his father landed on the side of his face.

"I ain't gon' tell you again. Get yo' ass back in your room! And don't come out until I tell you to! Now go!" Daquan didn't even wait to let his only son go back to his room. He immediately went over to Teresa and picked up where he left off, punishing her body with punches and kicks. He seemed oblivious to the fact that not only was he killing her, but also he was killing his unborn child right before his son's eyes.

A tear streamed down Genesis's face as he tried to reflect on one happy time he had with his dad, but he went blank. There were no happy times. From the first moment he could remember, his dad was a monster.

All Genesis remembered starting from the age of three was the constant beat downs his mother endured for no reason. If his dad's clothes weren't ironed just right, then a blow to the face. If the volume of the television was too loud, then a jab here. And, God forbid, if the small, two-bedroom apartment in the drug-infested building they lived in wasn't spotless, a nuclear bomb would explode in the form of Daquan. But the crazy part was, no matter how clean their apartment was or how good the food was cooked and his clothes being ironed just right, it was never good enough. Daquan would bust in the door, drunk or high, full of anger, ready to take out all his frustration out on his wife. The dead end jobs, being broke, living in the drug infested and violent prone city of Philadelphia had turned the already troubled man into poison to his whole family.

"Daddy, leave my mom alone," Genesis said in a calm, unemotional tone. Daquan kept striking Teresa as if he didn't hear his son. "I'm not gonna to tell you again. Leave my mom alone." This time Daquan heard his son's warning but seemed unfazed.

"I guess that swollen jaw wasn't enough for you. You dying to get that ass beat." Daquan looked down at a now black and blue Teresa who seemed to be about to take her last breath. "You keep yo' ass right here, while I teach our son a lesson." Teresa reached her hand out with the little strength she had left trying to save her son. But she quickly realized it was too late. The sins of the parents had now falling upon their child.

"Get away from my mother. I want you to leave and don't ever come back."

Daquan was so caught up in the lashing he had been putting on his wife that he didn't even notice Genesis retrieving the gun he left on the kitchen counter until he had it raised and pointed in his direction. "Lil' fuck, you un lost yo' damn mind! You gon' make me beat you with the tip of my gun."

Daquan reached his hand out to grab the gun out of Genesis's hand, and when he moved his leg forward, it would be the last step he'd ever take in his life. The single shot fired ripped through Daquan's heart and he collapsed on the kitchen floor, dying instantly.

Genesis was frozen and his mother began crying hysterically.

"Oh dear God!" Teresa moaned, trying to gasp for air. "Oh, Genesis baby, what have you done?" She stared at Daquan, who laid face up with his eyes wide open in shock. He died not believing until it was too late that his own son would be the one to take him out this world.

It wasn't until they heard the pounding on the front door that Genesis snapped back to the severity of the situation at hand.

"Is everything alright in there?" they heard the older lady from across the hall ask.

Genesis walked to the door still gripping the .380-caliber semi-automatic. He opened the door and said in a serene voice, "No, Ms. Johnson, everything is *not* alright. I just killed my father."

****

Two months later, Teresa cried as she watched her son being taking away to spend a minimum of two years in a juvenile facility in Pemberton, New Jersey.

Although it was obvious by the bruises on both Teresa and Genesis that he acted in self defense, the judge felt that the young boy having to live with the guilt of murdering his own father wasn't punishment enough. He concluded that if Genesis didn't get a hard wake up call, he would be headed on a path of self destruction. He first ordered him to stay at the juvenile facility until he was eighteen. But after pleas from his mother, neighbors and his teacher, who testified that Genesis had the ability to accomplish whatever he wanted in life because of how smart and gifted he was, the judge reduced it to two years, but only if he demonstrated excellent behavior during his time there. Those two years turned into four and four turned into seven. At the age of eighteen when Genesis was finally released he was no longer a young boy, he was now a criminal minded man.

ORDER FORM

Name:

Address:

City/State:

Zip:

QUANTITY	TITLES	PRICE	TOTAL
	Bitch	$15.00	
	Bitch Reloaded	$15.00	
	The Bitch Is Back	$15.00	
	Queen Bitch	$15.00	
	Last Bitch Standing	$15.00	
	Superstar	$15.00	
	Ride Wit' Me	$12.00	
	Ride Wit' Me Part 2	$15.00	
	Stackin' Paper	$15.00	
	Trife Life To Lavish	$15.00	
	Trife Life To Lavish II	$15.00	
	Stackin' Paper II	$15.00	
	Rich or Famous	$15.00	
	Rich or Famous Part 2	$15.00	
	Rich or Famous Part 3	$15.00	
	Bitch A New Beginning	$15.00	
	Mafia Princess Part 1	$15.00	
	Mafia Princess Part 2	$15.00	
	Mafia Princess Part 3	$15.00	
	Mafia Princess Part 4	$15.00	
	Mafia Princess Part 5	$15.00	
	Boss Bitch	$15.00	
	Baller Bitches Vol. 1	$15.00	
	Baller Bitches Vol. 2	$15.00	
	Baller Bitches Vol. 3	$15.00	
	Bad Bitch	$15.00	
	Still The Baddest Bitch	$15.00	
	Power	$15.00	
	Power Part 2	$15.00	
	Drake	$15.00	
	Drake Part 2	$15.00	
	Female Hustler	$15.00	
	Female Hustler Part 2	$15.00	
	Female Hustler Part 3	$15.00	
	Female Hustler Part 4	$15.00	
	Female Hustler Part 5	$15.00	
	Female Hustler Part 6	$15.00	
	Princess Fever "Birthday Bash"	$6.00	
	Nico Carter The Men Of The Bitch Series	$15.00	
	Bitch The Beginning Of The End	$15.00	
	Supreme...Men Of The Bitch Series	$15.00	
	Bitch The Final Chapter	$15.00	
	Stackin' Paper III	$15.00	
	Men Of The Bitch Series And The Women Who Love Them	$15.00	
	Coke Like The 80s	$15.00	
	Baller Bitches The Reunion Vol. 4	$15.00	
	Stackin' Paper IV	$15.00	
	The Legacy	$15.00	
	Lovin' Thy Enemy	$15.00	
	Stackin' Paper V	$15.00	
	The Legacy Part 2	$15.00	
	Assassins - Episode 1	$11.00	
	Assassins - Episode 2	$11.00	
	Assassins - Episode 2	$11.00	
	Bitch Chronicles	$40.00	
	So Hood So Rich	$15.00	
	Stackin' Paper VI	$17.99	

Shipping/Handling (Via Priority Mail) $7.50 1-2 Books, $15.00 3-4 Books add $1.95 for ea. Additional book.
Total: $_____FORMS OF ACCEPTED PAYMENTS: Certified or government issued checks and money Orders, all mail in orders take 5-7 Business days to be delivered

CPSIA information can be obtained
at www.ICGtesting.com
Printed in the USA
LVHW032305120421
684248LV00008B/153